Idols and Axle Grease

Idols
and
Axle Grease

Francis Irby Gwaltney

G.K.HALL&CO.

 Boston, Massachusetts

1975

56948

Library of Congress Cataloging in Publication Data

Gwaltney, Francis Irby.
    Idols and axle grease.

    "Published in large print."
    1.   Sight-saving books.   I.   Title.
[PZ4.G994Id3]   [PS3557.R2915]   813'.5'4   74-32305
ISBN 0-8161-6268-9

Illustrations by Barbara Norris

Published in Large Print by arrangement with The Bobbs-Merrill Company, Inc.

Set in Photon 18 pt Crown

This novel is dedicated to
Robert L. Morris

APOLOGIA

Sometimes this is a novel and then sometimes it isn't. Miss Doll, for instance, was real. Quite real. And Will Bumpers, whose youngest son was elected to his first term as governor of Arkansas in 1970, was killed in an automobile accident in 1949. There are others: Barney Stittchen, Clyde Hyatt, et al. But there is a lot of fiction mixed into all of this too. The only ones who will know truth from fiction are those from that loving little town, Charleston. It is somehow convincing to hear that if our country had had more Charlestons, there would never have been a Watergate.

Idols and Axle Grease

Norris   Miss Doll

I

She lay there, tiny, frail as a poorly remembered dream, unable to do justice to that rigid hospital bed so monumental beneath her small presence. An attendant, the employee of this "nursing home" in which she lay, stood at the foot of the bed, roundly inhibiting my conversation.

But that tiny woman in the bed wasn't inhibited. She never had been. Those interminable days of pencils and books and chalkboards had not even impressed her. Fifty years of a life that was supposed to have ended when she was hardly more than an infant and she had spent all of it cajoling, pleading, commanding, sometimes petting, but all of it loving. No irate principal ever came to her classroom demanding the company of some Onion Creek rowdy; she didn't believe in corporal punishment, so she wouldn't allow students to be taken out for punishment: save that for the study hall periods. There had been a long line of those men she had stood down on such an issue: principals, superintendents, school board members, parents — almost as many, she had once mused, as there had been of us students — and not a one of them ever buffaloed her.

When we were bright, she teased us. When we were stupid, she shamed us. Between those extremes lay a wonderful surplus of whim. We never really knew what position she might take. We really didn't care. It was sort of like the way Windy Spears put it: "It takes a good woman to make you like whatever she has to say." And that is the kind of woman she was. A good one.

Her classroom wasn't one of those places decorated with dusty pictures of Shakespeare or with slickly printed quotations from the English poets. (I shall never go to England while April is there.) That classroom was spartan: thirty student desks, her desk, three walls of chalkboards, one wall of windows. It smelled of young bodies and feet and of that peculiarly musky something the Onion Creek rowdies brought to town with them.

There was no sadness of pencils there. No tedium was there, either. Nor lethargy, ennui. There was a crackle in the air. She didn't like adverbs, because their use meant that somebody had chosen a weak verb or a small adjective. Long before people in Charleston ever heard of Winston Churchill, she told us that a preposition at the end of a sentence was something up with which she would not put. She almost jeered at those people we used as poets until our country got around to producing some real ones. She called them John the Greenleaf Whittier,

Ralph the Waldo Emerson, Henry the Wadsworth Longfellow.

Nor did she become hysterical in the presence of those poets she did like. She was loftily disdainful concerning the thing dull teachers called High Seriousness. She knew dozens of limericks and she could recite them by heart if it seemed to her that the Depression outside might be about to find its way into her classroom. Some of those limericks were mildly risqué: "There was a young fellow named Clyde, who fell in an outhouse and died. . . ."

She didn't know how to be impersonal. Indeed, the only impersonal teacher in Charleston High School had a big nose and wore jack-off bumps on his forehead. She, her tiny spine twisted, her neck inflexible, could somehow walk down those oiled floors of the hallways with a six-foot rowdy from Onion Creek, and, one arm about his waist and the other busy with a kind of cheerful gesturing, she could make him listen. Really listen. Of course the rowdy writhed, but not with embarrassment or humiliation or shame,

4

but with a pleasure as pure as any of the few we knew during the Depression.

Sometimes in her classroom, without pausing during a lecture, she whipped out a handkerchief and removed a pencil mark from some face straining with understanding. The student knew what to do when she stopped before him: he stuck out his tongue, she wet her handkerchief on it, and the pencil mark was whisked away. Without giving pause to that rush of words, I have seen her comb and plait the long, heavy hair of one of the girls while the girl bent over a tablet and took notes.

She never passed my desk that she didn't brush my hair away from my forehead. She also managed to lightly touch my shoes with one of her own shoes; I was the shine boy at the Star Barber Shop and she was forever amused by the fact that I steadfastly refused to wear bright shoes. Then, with another brush at my forehead, she was on her way, glancing at papers, correcting spelling, occasionally petting one of us who looked as if we might need affection.

She never gave up on my hair,

especially my forehead. My cowlick was an enormous fan of adolescent blondness, and I was the victim of endless joking about it; she alone liked it. She told Windy Spears that only a fool would fail to notice that I had a noble forehead, "Daniel Webster gothic." Windy didn't know what she was talking about, but he stopped teasing me about my hair.

The other day, as I knelt by that hospital bed, she brushed my hair away from my forehead and murmured, "Your forehead's a little more gothic than it was."

"Yessum, I guess it is."

There's no counting the students she had. She began teaching when she was still a teenager. She was an elementary teacher then. Third grade. When a vacancy occurred in "high school," a particularly persuasive superintendent of schools talked her into teaching grades seven through twelve, six classes of English a day and one study hall. Her study hall was as busy as a classroom; she would tackle any subject, and of course she wouldn't listen to any of us who said we didn't have time for our homework.

That energy came not from her body. Legend had it that she was dropped during her infancy, and in those days there was no physician who would have known what to do. She cried for weeks, it was said, and then slowly the back became deformed and the neck stiff. Somehow, she was a beautiful woman. Not really, of course: she taught us that John Milton was right when he said that extremes constitute ugliness. But she had style. Even when she swiveled her body at the hips, unable to turn her head, she did it with a style and a vitality that caused her contemporaries to appear dull.

That energy came from her spirit. (She taught us that Spirit was the social word, Soul the theological one.) And she wasn't above using that energy and that spirit to help relieve the mundane. In 1938, CHS had a football team that by all rights should have taken up knitting. The line was tall and heavy and the backfield was fast and tough, but that team was bedeviled by bad luck. We hadn't won a game in two years.

But that last game in 1939 was something else. There was a pep rally in our brand-new WPA gym, and our bepimpled, adenoidal cheerleaders were desperate in their efforts to make us believe that our team could win, could actually win if we would just get behind the boys with a couple or three rousing cheers. We wanted nothing to do with it.

I don't remember the cheers she decided to lead, but she walked out there on that flawlessly polished floor, her heels pecking, thus breaking the rule that bare feet, socks, and tennis shoes were all that were allowed, and ignoring her twisted spine and her rigid neck, she pranced and danced her way through some three or four cheers. When she was done, the WPA gym was bedlam. We won that game. Well — not really; we tied it. But that was so close that we called it a victory.

She was never paid as much as a hundred dollars a month. Even during World War II, when the shortage of men prompted the school board to finally recognize her genius and thus appoint her superintendent of schools, she wasn't offered the salary to go with the position. But for all her poverty, she had an extra dime for the paper boy when he collected for the Fort Smith paper that was delivered daily in Charleston, *The Southwest American*. Somehow, she could afford to stock first her icebox and then later her refrigerator with various kinds of goodies that would be a nice bite for her constant parade of visitors.

During World War II we were given furloughs before we were shipped abroad. We were supposed to visit our folks, but we called on her too. Older people remember that there were always sun-browned boys in khaki or olive drab in her parlor during that war, a cup and a saucer and a plate loaded with pie or cake balanced on knees that had seemed so knobby during the Depression but were strong and ready now. Because so many of us had only the education she had given us, most of us were infantrymen, but one of us became a pilot, Thumb Holyfield, and one of us, Topwater Mulligan, became an infantry officer. Even so, most of us were infantrymen, and thus Charleston's Roll of Honor was a long one. None of us left these shores without personal assurance of her love for us.

She wrote thousands of letters during the war. Because of the shortage of teachers, she taught eight classes instead of seven, even after she was appointed superintendent of schools, and every classroom was packed. That made no difference to her; there was a theme due every Friday. A book report was due the first Monday of every month. There is no counting the papers she marked during those years, but she replied promptly to every letter she received from us, and sometimes when we didn't keep up our end of the writing bargain, we received a sharply scolding note to set us right. But that was rare; she represented to us all that was good and right about Charleston, the things that caused Charleston to survive the Depression; thus we wrote to her in the same spirit that prompted us to keep in contact with parents and kinfolks.

Somehow she remembered us. In each letter there was always a private reference to something nobody but she could have known. More than a few of us died in that war, and there are dozens of parents in Charleston today who still have those letters because they were included in personal effects taken from bodies and shipped home by commanding officers.

The golden melancholia for that past isn't as dim as it might seem to people who are a part of a modern education system, a machine that produces the impersonal as if it were another equation in the GNP. There are hundreds of us who can remember, with considerable humor, "The stag at eve had drunk his fill,/Where danced the moon on Monan's rill" as the perfect example of iambic pentameter. We can also remember that such a poem, *The Lady of the Lake,* is pretty awful. One of us, our junior senator now and once the state's most popular governor, once said, his voice fraught with disgust, that most of the staff appointed to answer the hundreds of letters he receives each day could have profited immensely if that tiny, frail woman could have touched her wand to their foreheads when they were youngsters.

We know the difference between a simile and a metaphor, but we prefer the metaphor; there is something definitely positive about it. We know how to test the objective and the nominative. We know the linking verbs because we were taught that they were the strong ones. We know the levels of symbolism in *The Scarlet Letter,* but we also know that *Moby Dick* could — just could — have been a literary failure because it was a tract.

She didn't teach us that proper spelling was a virtue. There are dictionaries for that. It is the word itself that counts. She was polite to those people who won WPA spelling bees during the Depression, but she was quick to point out that the time memorizing those spellings could have been spent on a good, deeply entertaining novel, and the difference would have been remarkable.

She never assigned memory work in poetry either, but she knew hundreds of poems by heart. She shrugged — and with her spine and neck, that was indeed a florid gesture — and told us that we would remember poetry important to us. She was right; I remember a lot of Housman because I'm a sentimental man who sees the past through a diffuse golden haze in which nobody is ever correctly remembered.

She never trusted the memory experts. To fill one's mind with a vast array of trivia appalled her. Twenty years ago, when I published my first novel, I called upon her and mentioned that I relied upon notes rather than memory. She shook her head, another florid gesture, and said that I had made a serious mistake. Thus I shall use no notes here.

It was her memory that was last to go. After all those years, that spine and that neck put her to bed and kept her there. She lay in the orange light of a September afternon that found its way into the nursing home windows, and, lost in the vastness of a hospital bed that had never been designed with such as her in mind, she received another one of us who paraded by her bedside in such astonishing numbers. ''She cain't remember much that's happened since

56948

she left the schoolhouse," the attendant said, "but if she ever taught you, she'll remember."

I bent over her bed, and for a moment it seemed that the only heroine I had ever known wasn't going to know me. She adjusted her spectacles, peered, and then she frowned slightly. "The cowlick's gone," she said. "Now the entire world can see a noble forehead." And with a quick gesture, she pretended to brush my hair out of my eyes.

The voice hadn't changed at all. It was vital, vibrant; come to think of it, the badge of greatness might be a distinctive voice. It was taut, that voice, strong but not loud.

Her name was Laura Means. We called her Miss Doll because she was so pretty. She was born in 1884. She died in 1974. She was the first idol. The axle grease follows.

Windy
Spears

Norris

II

Windy Spears was a native of Charleston and, except for his service in France during what we then called the World's War and on another occasion a solitary trip to Little Rock, he had never been more than fifty miles from home. He came by his nickname honestly enough.

Windy lived on a pension, and because pensioned veterans were better off during the Depression than at any time in our history, he lived well. His house was painted every third year, and because that gleaming whiteness contrasted so sharply with the shabby gray of houses that hadn't been painted since 1929, it looked like a mansion. It was filled with children: Miz Spears, a compactly built little woman who had been a Sipes as a maiden, established herself as a champion during the early and middle twenties — she had a baby every eleven months. Most of them were big, heavy boys. Since each baby added something to the size of Windy's pension, and since Doc Bollinger delivered babies for a fee of ten dollars, and because Windy's wife and children raised most of the family's food in that three-acre vegetable garden behind the house, Windy didn't find children an expensive luxury.

Windy was a man of habit. He arose at 5:30, ate a ham steak and four basted eggs with grits and five cups of coffee, then went to town, a block away. He carried a cane as a part of his disability, although he had been gassed and there was nothing wrong with his legs. At the corner of Main Street — hereafter cited as the Street —

and North Greenwood Street, he picked up a bottle cap from a supply washed into the storm drain by the rains, then he used his cane as a club. He could knock that bottle cap sailing. It always landed between the regular and ethyl pumps of Melmer Dunmore's Filling Station. Then he called on Melmer.

Windy didn't stay long. He, like everybody else in Charleston, didn't like Melmer. It's just that Melmer's establishment was en route to better things, and besides, Melmer willingly listened to Windy's lies.

At the Tourist Cafe, Windy had a cup of coffee. That required almost an hour, because Dock Frye, proprietor, was still serving breakfast to Onion Creek rowdies in town after having sold their produce; thus the conversation was often interrupted. Windy was fond of Dock because he obviously believed any lie anybody wanted to tell him.

The hotel, really a room-and-board, was Windy's destination. There he could spend almost any number of comfortable hours with the proprietor, Old Cat Murphy.

They had been sweethearts when they were young, and early in the Depression, when Old Cat was still a widder woman, sometimes they would even flirt — wanly, of course.

Old Cat had become mildly sophisticated from having been in contact with those occasional travelers who alighted at the hotel overnight; thus she had a developed talent for making Windy feel as if he might not be entirely appreciated in Charleston. Old Cat was also the only person in Charleston who could call Windy a liar without hurting his feelings.

"You're a liar and the truth ain't in you, Windy Spears." Old Cat's grin was kind of soft and regular. "You'd lie on credit if you knew you could git cash for the truth."

Windy shrugged; he really didn't care. " 'Spect so."

"Even Miss Doll don't believe you, and she'll believe anybody."

Windy settled comfortably; he knew Miss Doll loved him. "Well — I tell you, Cat, a man's gotta do something he gits a kick out of and ain't nothing sets me afire like a well-told lie."

Windy went home for lunch, and, surrounded by his battalion of children and his sturdy, uncomplaining wife, he related his adventures of the morning. That wife was one of those women who used her husband as both a symbol and a weapon, so to his children Windy was a tyrant to whom young people listened with rigid respect. It was easier that way; when on those four occasions he was obliged to use his razor strop on one of those monumental sons, the experience put him to bed for a solid week. Even the third son, he who became one of the first All-Americans produced by the University of Arkansas Razorbacks, didn't talk back to his father.

There was a nap after lunch, and then, at 1:30, Windy continued with his routine. That meant an hour of gospel singing at the cobbler's shop, Spreading Adder Benefield, Prop. It was a quartet, with Spread singing bass, J. O. Cone at baritone, Barney Stittchen at tenor, and Windy at top tenor. To judges of gospel singing, Windy was considered to be one of the best top tenors in Franklin County, north or south of the river. Indeed, the quartet had once sung a few nervous hymns on KFPW Fort Smith, and Windy was invited, via letter and even telephone, to join several groups and quartets who had commercial aspirations.

Thus Windy's life was serene. It was easy talk, satisfying song, and a firm domestic tradition. None of us were complaining listeners. We all knew he had never seen combat during the World's War; he was in a quartermaster outfit several miles behind the trenches and a canister of phosgene exploded. Windy somehow took a whiff or so before he recognized his error. We all knew that. So did Windy. But we never said so. The tales Windy told were such monumental lies that they were first class entertainment in an era when the Gem Theater was open only two nights a week.

I was never taught that Windy told the truth. My mother was crazy. She ambled about our tiny house and our small yard, and people pitied her and swore I was going to hell for raising myself with no father and a crazy mother. I was never taught that Windy was a liar. I didn't need to be.

I had good instincts.

So it wasn't I, nor was it any one of us who called Windy's hand. It was a stranger, that most contemptible of people during the Depression, a Yankee with a hard voice and eyes lighter than the color of his face. He was an engineer employed by the WPA to build a viaduct over the railroad at Doctor's Ford Creek. That engineer stayed at the hotel, and when he wasn't trying to make time with Miss Hettie McIntosh, he was trying the same thing with Old Cat Murphy. Perhaps it was pure malice or perhaps it was simply jealousy when Old Cat stopped her bottom-wiggling and her lisping and her lip-licking in the presence of Windy — it made no difference because the engineer wanted Old Cat and he hated Windy.

While the engineer simmered and Old Cat listened, Windy made his daily call. Old Cat never accused him of lying in the presence of either friends or strangers, and because Windy knew he was safe, he put on a better show at the hotel than he did at, say, the filling station or the cobbler's shop.

Events conspired against Windy but they didn't defeat him. The subject of this morning's talk just happened to match an event that has yet to be forgotten in the gentle flow of Charleston's history. "They chased that old boy all over France," Windy was saying. "Finally they holed him up in one of them old French castles. Châteauseases, the French called 'em. Well, Lord knows, the MPs carried billy clubs; they didn't know how to use a rifle. So they come to my colonel and said they needed a man with rifle experience, one that could drive a five-penny nail from fifty feet, one that's owned a rifle all his life. Well, my colonel — old Colonel Winfield from out here at Vesta; he died last winter and I was head guard at his funeral. Well, Colonel picked me and some old boy from Tulsa, Oklahoma, but that Tulsa boy couldn't make it; in fact, he died with the flu. So that left it up to me."

The WPA engineer didn't believe a word of it, and he had his mouth cocked to say so, but Windy kept a fast pace; thus the engineer didn't get his chance.

"I'll tell you right now, I was scared, but that feller in the château had done a lot of killing, women and children mostly, and everybody was getting excited, so I didn't have no choice. I had to get 'im. It taken a while, almost all day, but I done it. I didn't want to kill a feller American, so I had to get in a position where I could shoot his gun outta his hand. So I —"

The telephone rang, and in Charleston in 1938 a ringing telephone meant something. The phone was an upright attached to one of those accordion extensions, which meant that it could telescope as much as six feet into a room. Old Cat nodded to the engineer, who relinquished his contempt for Windy long enough to shove the phone at Old Cat. As a part of her sophistication she had developed her own distinctive way of answering the phone, "Mmm, neh-low. . . ." And she listened.

Windy continued with his story, because even if the engineer wasn't paying close attention now, he was in the room and Windy had an audience.

Old Cat shoved the phone back to the engineer. "Just a minute, Windy." In another town and in another state, that would have meant this: Shut up and listen. But in Charleston we were rarely rude to one another.

Windy hushed; he wasn't angry, nor were his feelings hurt. He knew Old Cat had heard something awful on that telephone or she would never have asked him to stop talking.

Old Cat went to the window and looked down the Street. "They'uz two men holding up the bank right now. That'uz Dock Frye looking for Pete McCarthy," our sheriff.

The engineer recoiled and muttered something ugly, but Windy, still enraptured perhaps by the delicious violence inherent in the tale he had been telling, said, "Now just take it easy." His voice had the artificial clarity of the sleepwalker's.

The engineer didn't hesitate. He stepped behind the desk and picked up a shotgun

Old Cat kept there. He threw it to Windy, who had completely recovered his native cowardice by now and thus dropped the shotgun. Dazed, he picked it up. The engineer shoved a box of shells across the desk, and then he fetched up a .45 automatic Old Cat kept under the cash box.

"All right, loudmouth," the engineer said, "now's the time for you to either put up or shut up. I got a real fast Lincoln car and there's plenty of room on the fender for you to lay and use that shotgun."

Windy's voice was thin and horribly reedy: "I get a pension." And because he had produced what was generally considered a good excuse for inaction, he took a small breath of relief.

"Yeah, for being the biggest liar in the World's War." The engineer shoved Windy toward the door. "Now you going with me or do I find a real man?"

Windy later confessed to Old Cat and, indeed, to me that he didn't really remember leaving the hotel, and sure enough, when he installed himself, rather tentatively, on the fender of the Lincoln, he was gray with a fear that must have been near death, but somehow he poked the barrel of the shotgun between the fender and the right headlight.

That was when the robbers emerged from the bank. They fired several shots up and down the Street, and then they jumped into their Model A, a blue one with a rumble seat and a cloth top, and then they hurried on out of town. Windy flinched when the engineer fired up the Lincoln, and if he hadn't been quick to grab the headlight, Windy would have fallen off.

It might not have been a shooting match at all if the bank robbers hadn't turned left at Schoolhouse Hill. No children were injured; indeed, we paid no attention to the robbers at all, because the first bell had already rung and we were busy at play, getting in four more minutes before the second bell rang for books. One of the games the boys were playing was Pile, and to Windy it appeared as if several boys were grouped anxiously about somebody who had fallen before the robbers' guns. That was when Windy got hold of himself.

The robbers were overtaken when they crossed the tracks near the old Spessard place. It was a rough crossing and the driver lost control on the dirt road for perhaps twenty-five yards. He used his brakes, and the engineer rammed his Lincoln almost against the Model A's bumper. That was when, no more than twenty feet from his target, Windy fired his first shot.

The robbers fired back; Windy didn't have an easy time of it. He was unwounded, but the engineer caught a buckshot slug in his left thigh. The Lincoln's radiator was wrecked and steaming. Windy told me and Old Cat that he began figuring, right then, that he'd better shoot fast and straight or that Model A was going to leave the Lincoln behind. His next two shots did the trick.

Nobody was killed, and that made our history a little easier to bear. The robbers were taken to Doc Bollinger's hospital, and something like a hundred pellets of number six duckload were removed from their necks and scalps. The *Fort Smith*

Times Record and *The Southwest American* sent a photographer down, and, watched by our entire population, Windy was pictured returning the money to Clyde Hiatt at the bank. Another picture showed him, still holding the shotgun, in the company of his compact little wife and all those children.

The event changed the pattern of Windy's life. He never embellished upon the tale, and he was always quick to admit that he had been frightened out of his wits. Later, when he was no longer a hero but was instead that consumptive-looking little man with bright eyes who talked a lot, he refused to talk about the robbery at all.

"Why don't you ever want to talk about it anymore, Windy?"

He looked at me as if I were a fool. "You ever been shot at, boy?"

"No sir."

"Well, it ain't no fun." Windy mused a moment. "A man ain't fixing to get shot at for telling a little lie or two."

"No sir." I waited because I knew he had something else to say.

"If you or anybody else wants to know the truth about it, it'uz in the newspapers and it's been framed and hung in the courthouse. That's all anybody ever needs to know about it."

And as he grew older, another war produced younger men who came home to lie about their own military careers. Windy became something of a listener, and even when he was absolutely certain that these new liars were not made of that substantial old-fashioned cloth of his generation, he encouraged them, nodded at the right times, asked the right questions; he was, to the really good liars of the new generation, a father figure. It was a role he relished almost as much as the one he had played when he had pioneered twentieth-century lying in Charleston.

When he died, finally a victim of that phosgene accident, he left various mementoes of his life to his friends in Charleston. Colonel Pettibone received the campaign hat. The shoes went to Scrooge Wilkins. Spread Benefield, for one reason or another, got the gas mask.

The mess kit went to Will Bumpers. I'll never know why he decided to leave me the rifle.

Windy was given a soldier's funeral. It was the biggest funeral Charleston had ever seen. The American Legion was out en masse, officious, their silly uniforms somehow appropriate, their perfect attendance medals ajingle. Even the governor attended. But the perfect touch was a complete surprise; somebody lost in that maze called the Veterans Administration must have known Windy, because when his tombstone was produced, it failed to list the military organization to which Windy had belonged. The Quartermaster Corps, some sentimental bureaucrat reasoned, couldn't have produced a man like Jasper Sue "Windy" Spears, so after his name came the simple words "United States Infantry."

With Spreading Adder Benefield in charge, a gospel quartet sang several hymns over Windy's grave. Windy had had no favorite hymn, but Spread did;

thus the featured hymn was "Shout the Glad Tidings." We all agreed that the tune seemed right enough.

Spread
Benefield   Norris

III

During the Depression, Charleston could easily support two cobblers, because a decent pair of shoes cost as much as three dollars, and repair continued as long as sole and uppers held together. Both cobblers — one long ago lost in the terror called Time — enjoyed a certain prosperity: they both owned automobiles and both were plump.

Spreading Adder Benefield, indeed, found himself named by his prosperity.

He was a stocky man, strong of arm and stout of leg, but it was his stomach that named him. It pointed ahead of him with a sort of resolute bulge, and as he made his pacific rounds it swayed, heaved, and wagged with a placid kind of determination that would remain with him until his death. It was Windy Spears who put the nickname on Spreading Adder.

Spread was a religious man. Baptist. He was known to have used unusual language only once in his entire life, and then he had said an ugly word to the wife of one of those Baptist preachers who arrived and departed with some regularity during the Depression.

Spread was the organizing spirit behind a thousand Singing Conventions. But it was Summer Singing School he liked best. He closed his shop mornings during Singing School and drove his sparkling Model T to the Baptist Church and spent four solid hours, without pause, teaching the fun and mystery of shaped notes, *do re me fa sol la te do,* calling the notes aloud as he sang along in his curiously reedy bass-baritone until the summer's crop of teenagers knew them and how to use them.

Perhaps Spread and I became friends — if a middle-aged man and a teenage shine boy can be friends — when I closed my shine stand at the barber shop and went to Summer Singing School. No matter what kind of trouble I got into after that, Spread refused to believe that there was anybody but God in my heart.

The unrelenting summers, curiously enough, aren't remembered for their brassy heat and smoldering armpits; most of us do remember, however, Spread's Summer Singing School. We sang "God Has Blotted Them Out" and "Shall We Gather at the River" and "Jordan's Stormy Banks" and one outstandingly horrible one called "Before Jehovah's Awful Throne," which continued after its title phrase with "Ye nations bow with sacred joy: Know that the Lord is God Alone; He can create and He can destroy." Some of us remember the terror of the Trinity with greater clarity than we do the heat, but perhaps we remember Spread with greater love than we do the Trinity.

He was a native of Charleston, the son of a man the same and a grandfather and a great-grandfather the same, he who came to Charleston in the early nineteenth century and founded it at the confluence of Onion Creek and Tater Hill Run. All of them had been cobblers and all wore those strangely marsupial pouches of fat over their stomachs. They even married the same kinds of women, small, silent, affectionate, fertile, and religious. Baptists. All of them were Baptists. Until Spread married, the Benefield wives had all been altos, but his wife's voice should have warned him; she was more tenor than alto. A male tenor could be intensely fertile — witness Windy Spears — but a woman wasn't supposed to be a tenor. Spread's wife was barren.

Thus Spread wasn't a happy man. The lack of children didn't bother him when he was still a young man because the Lord giveth and He also makes it a point to occasionally take away, but now that Spread was in his early fifties, the Lord appeared to have given him hardly anything at all. There were a few jokes among us: Amil Curzon, Charleston's iceman who could produce twins with great ease, offered to pitch in and help. Spread smiled; he smiled a lot. He knew his wife was kind of pretty. But there was a sort of soft edge to that smile, as if perhaps Spread sometimes cried when he was assured of privacy.

My shine stand was directly across the Street, and I was there to learn the principles of that vice and virtue called, for want of an honest name, free enterprise. Often enough, especially in the late summer when Singing School was over and the two barbers were asleep in their chairs, I crossed the Street and watched and listened while Spread guarded against the degeneration of Charleston's shoes.

If the quartet wasn't singing, Spread was always busy. "Just set there, boy, and I'll be right along with you."

"I don't want anything, Mr. Benefield. I just want to watch you work."

Spread was pleased. "Much oblige."

Spread had good hands and he was proud of them. And when he was pleased, he knew how to please shine boys too. "I didn't think you'd need to have them Friendly Fives fixed just yet."

"No sir, not yet." Friendly Fives were popular in western Arkansas during the Depression because they were handsomely pointed at the toe and they cost five dollars. The only pair in town belonged to Raymond Frye, a busy cornet player in Lum Lively's Uptown Orchestra at Fort Smith and Other Great American Cities.

While Spread worked, he either sang or whistled. His whistle wasn't really a whistle; it was a sturdy hiss of controlled frequency, thus he could hiss a good tune without sounding like some kind of mocking bird. His voice, at song, was something else; it was loud, albeit reedy, deep, and he was proud of it. Above the rattle of his machinery, he cleared his throat a couple of times the same way Dock Frye did before he disposed of a schooner of Falstaff, and then Spread sang. He knew the *New Baptist Hymnal* by heart, but he preferred those tunes written in 6/8 time because he could speed them up without their sounding blasphemous. One of his favorites was "True-Hearted, Whole-Hearted" because the last phrase went "Peal out the watchword! Loyal forever!" He could make the Street ring on hot summer afternoons with those words.

Had it not been for his music, Spread's life might have been dismal. A barren wife for a man who loved children. Will Bumpers had the hardware store next door and sometimes Spread talked to him, but Will was really close to nobody. Nor was Spread, but immediately beneath the lake calm of his life lay a great affection. Will and Spread sometimes hummed a few bars of a hymn, but Will was a Methodist, not really a singer. I was a Methodist too, but even if I did play upright alto in Barney Stittchen's American Legion Band, and even if I could read shaped notes with all the ease in the world, I did no more for the pattern of Spread's life than Will Bumpers did. The only real love in the life of Spread

Benefield was the quartet, and that was, until one afternoon, a mild love at that.

That was during the summer of 1936. It was a day no hotter, not really different, no cleaner than any other day in any other summer, but during that afternoon came a crisis philosophers like to talk about. Spread's life changed. So did the lives of the rest of us.

The event was probably illegal, perhaps even criminal under those legal codes we still called a democracy, but this was the sort of thing we didn't argue with. Probably because we really didn't care.

It wasn't the first load of orphans to pass through Charleston, but it was the first to arrive in a bus. In the past, trains of fifteen to twenty cars laden with orphans came through hundreds of small towns in the mid-South, leaving a boy here or a girl somewhere else until, finally, the train was empty. There was a "fee" attached to each "adoption."

The bus was parked in front of Spread's shop. It made quite a racket when it stopped, because it was equipped with the new air brakes, and the quartet — Barney

Stittchen, J. O. Cone, Windy Spears, and Spread — was disturbed enough that Windy went to the door to see why a bus would be arriving in Charleston in the middle of a bristling August afternoon, but there was no stopping of the hymn in progress, "A Glory Gilds the Sacred Page." I stayed at the door, and when I saw what might be inside that bus, I stopped my almost silent humming of the tune.

The sponsor of the orphan bus was no stranger to Charleston. He had been making at least two passes through this part of Arkansas since early in the twenties, and he kept it up until Governor Bailey put a stop to it in 1939. He glanced once into the shoe shop, giving me that peculiarly vapid look con men give to young people who see through them but can't hurt them, and then he hurried on down the Street. He hurried because Charleston was saturated as a market; we were a fertile people, and we were moral enough that we didn't like to pay a "fee" for help intended for the fields.

The children in the bus were silent, as

silent as that truckload of convicts had been when it had stopped for water the week before. Indeed, the only sound on the Street during that bristling afternoon was the quartet. They were trying a new one, "Shout the Glad Tidings," and they were having trouble with it. Not that there weren't shaped notes. It wasn't that at all. The tune was easy too, but it was written in 6/4 time and it had two refrains, one at the beginning and one at the end.

Windy Spears wagged his head with dismal desperation. "Hod-damn, boys, the feller that wrote that tune must of been on a dram." Windy looked to see who had written the music. "W. A. Mühlenberg. Well, if I'd of been named Mühlenberg, I'd of probably messed it up too. Turn the machine off, Spread, and let's get 'er worked out so's we'n move on to the next tune."

The four men huddled about their hymnals and went to work, but they didn't know how to handle the 6/4 time. Spread figured it was a mistake, and they tried it in 6/8. That worked, but it didn't sound like anything they had ever heard before, and in Charleston we didn't like anything we weren't accustomed to. It was during that sweaty silence while they pondered the problem of 6/4 time that they were interrupted.

Two voices, both child sopranos and singing in a language none of us had ever heard before, sang ''Shout the Glad Tidings'' the way it was supposed to be sung. The quartet immediately came to the door and listened. The singing was, of course, coming from the bus.

All of us were moved to tears by the music, but Spread was almost sobbing. In a dusty little town in western Arkansas on a hot summer afternoon, the ugliness of his barren life had suddenly become unbearable. It was Windy Spears who had control enough to speak. ''Hod-damn, them two little old girls sound like a couple of regular mockingbirds.''

When the two children finished the hymn, Spread moved with a kind of ponderous preoccupation toward the bus and jerked the door open. I was on the sidewalk, some fifteen feet away, and I felt the rush of heat that gushed from that bus when the door was opened. There was a kind of a wail from inside and a collective murmur that sounded to us like they had all said in unison, "Dunky," and then they, all of the children, began singing "Shout the Glad Tidings."

It wasn't in English. An English hymn couldn't have been so beautiful. It was some kind of foreign language, and none of us had ever heard such clarity of beauty. Spread, never a resolute man at all, didn't hesitate: he entered the bus and, gently pressing the children, urged them into the comparative cool beneath the wooden canopy in front of Spread's shop. The children, the oldest no more than twelve and the youngest no less than eight, didn't stop singing.

Dirty, staggering with exhaustion, those children stood erect on the sidewalk and, sort of like little soldiers, sang with a roundness of note that belied their appearance. As they sang, Spread passed from one to another and listened until he found the two who had begun the singing. They were girls, a set of stocky twins, blonde, and even if they were hollow of eye and tottering with fatigue, their voices, when Spread urged them toward more volume, rose like the music of angels is said to have once done.

The singing stopped. When it began again, it wasn't music anybody in Charleston had ever heard before. We weren't even sure it was a hymn. The voices weren't so strong this time either; those children were weak with hunger and thirst. Spread passed from one of the children to the next, touching cheeks and foreheads.

"Every one of these cheern's running a temperature," Spread said, as if perhaps he couldn't understand that it was considerably hotter in that bus than it was here under the canopy.

Windy Spears eased up to me and murmured, " 'Spect you'd best see if Doc Bollinger's in his office, boy."

Doc was, and he listened patiently before he stepped to the door and called across the Street, "I'm right here, y'all." Doc ambled across the Street with a kind of stolid impatience and grabbed the first of the children he reached. It didn't take

44

him long. "Get the kids something to drink and some sugar too. Lemonade. Lots of lemonade. Sugar cookies."

There is no telling how so many people gathered about that bus so quickly. Charleston owned 853 people in the census of 1930, but most of them had already gone to California by now. On that hot afternoon it looked as if perhaps as many as 500 people had suddenly appeared. Claude Jones, a sort of a pleasant and bumbling man, didn't ask for money; he was our grocer and he had lemons and sugar. J. O. Cone got the cookies from his own store. Will Bumpers furnished a number-three galvanized washtub from his hardware store. Amil Curzon brought the ice, and within minutes those children were drinking and eating.

There was no shyness on the part of the children. They concentrated on it. They worked at it. Spread sat on the curb, watching, murmuring encouragement, and occasionally one of the children gave him a tentative little poke in the ribs or a shy touch on the shoulder. A couple of the younger boys took up with Windy Spears.

When the twin girls sat at his feet and gorged themselves on cookies and lemonade, Spread let himself cry without inhibition. He didn't howl or sob; he simply cried. He was a happy man. The twins teased him by prodding that placid pouch that lay over his stomach.

There were eleven children, and two of them vomited because they couldn't take care of the sugar, but Doc urged them on, and soon enough they had refilled themselves. It was at this moment of the bristling afternoon's tableau that the bus, a few feet away, was forgotten, and that was when the sponsor crept into his machine, and with a great hiss of brakes and another roar of the engine he drove away.

If we had saved the lives of eleven children, that was one thing. Now there were homeless children in town. That was something else.

It couldn't have become an issue, because we were all taken by the beauty of their voices, but it could have been an emergency. Two of the children were cripples, and there was the issue of not separating the twins.

Spread handled that. He stood on the curb and, squinting into the falling yellow sun, lifted his voice to reason with us. He had never sounded so dignified before. "I aim to take the best two and the worst two. Them two twin girls and them two crippled little boys. Y'all can have the rest of 'em long's you don't aim to make hired hands out of 'em." Spread sort of shrugged. "They cain't talk our talk but they'n shore sing." And for the first time in his life, perhaps even for the last time, Spread made a feeble attempt toward a kind of humor. "I always wanted me a quartet at home."

Windy Spears promptly stepped up and took the hand of one of the girls. "Thus'un's mine." He pointed to another girl: "I'll take that'un too if none y'all's got dibbies on'er."

The remaining children were gone within seconds.

Spread ponderously herded his four into his shop. There he stopped and peered back at me. "Boy . . .?"

I entered the shop. "Yes sir?"

Spread was a satisfied man, but he had made the longest step in his life, and he wasn't sure how it would be handled when he got home. "Did you hear them kids singing?" He knew I had been there.

"Yes sir."

"Purty, wudn't it, boy?"

"Yes sir, it was."

"*Well* . . ." Spread looked at the four children, and then he absently patted his pockets as if he were looking for perhaps a pipe to smoke or a little chewing tobacco, but Spread didn't use the stuff in any form. "*Well!*"

"Yes sir," I said. "Mr. Benefield, if there's anything you need me to do . . ."

Spread almost grinned; almost, but not quite. Then it seemed as if he might be ready to cry. "Boy, I'm fixing to go on home with four cheern my wife never laid eyes on."

"Let 'em sing for'er, Mr. Benefield," I said. "She'll like 'em."

"Probably." But Spread wasn't ready to go on home yet. "Mmm," he said to the children.

They eased into a corner, and somehow

or other they all knew he loved them but wasn't quite ready to brag about it yet. They sat and looked at him, their hands folded before them, their faces small and placid. When I had time to think back on it, those four children looked as if Spread were their natural father.

Spread looked down at my shoes. I took some pride in them: they never looked shined. And they were the cheapest pair of clodhoppers I could find. They weren't at all the kind of shoes Spread pretended they were. "How'd you like a pair of steel taps on them Friendly Fives of yours, boy?" There was another pair of Friendly Fives now and they belonged to Scrooge Wilkins, but nothing in my imagination ever prompted me to think I would ever own a pair.

"Well, boy, I got a chore for you —"

"Yes sir." It wasn't a question; I knew what he needed me for.

"I'm a needing you to help me get these cheern home," Spread said. "I don't figger I can just stumble in with four brand-new cheern."

"No sir, 'spect not."

"Then you'll help me, you're saying?"

"I'm saying yes, Mr. Benefield."

Spread felt as if he should explain. "My woman's a good wife all the time and better the rest of the time, but she ain't gave me no babies."

"Yes sir."

Somebody must have warned Spread's wife. She met Spread and me and her four new children with tears and food, the only sure way of making a welcome obvious. She kissed us all, though I didn't particularly relish being kissed at that particular moment.

We never knew where the children came from. Perhaps Spread knew; perhaps even Windy. But they never told and we never asked. We did learn, as World War II drew nearer, that their native language had been German, and we closed our ranks against the possibility that somebody might persecute them, but nobody ever said a word against those children.

Dramaturgy would demand that at least one of the children would find an insufferable flaw in Charleston's society.

None ever did. One of them, Pudd Jarrell, was no good, but that was a better average than any of us had ever hoped for. Even so, Pudd was no good because he was — well — no good. Somehow or other he was redeemed, because he was killed during the Battle of the Bulge.

One other of the children was killed, this one at the Battle of Buna Mountain. Spread erected monuments to both of them, and those monuments still stand on that bald eminence that used to be a forested knoll which we called Nixon Graveyard.

It would be nice to report that those singing twins went on to great success. They didn't. Neither went to college. Nor did the one Windy Spears took home. Not a one of them went to college. Not a one ever learned anything else about music except shaped notes.

Indeed, it wasn't until Spreading Adder Benefield died that the survivors of the eleven felt so close that they thought they should again assemble as they had under the wooden awning in front of Spread's shop. Until his funeral, on a simmering

Sunday in 1954 when I was far too old to play Taps on my aging cornet, those children didn't get together at all, because there were other things they had to do with their adopted brothers and sisters.

Windy Spears got them together. Windy would have assembled mourners for — say — even Melmer Dunmore, but this was something special. He got them together at the Baptist Church and they practiced "Shout the Glad Tidings," but now their experience was too far removed to do the hymn well. Finally, before defeat expelled them, they sang through those hymns they had known all their adult lives, and that is the music that was heard over Spread's coffin. Only the twins and the two cripples could manage an arrangement of "Shout the Glad Tidings," and even so, they didn't do too well by it.

Windy Spears, weeping broadly, stood between the twins as one of them, pregnant with her seventh baby, spoke Spread's epitaph. "We was his cheern twenty years. Nobody could ever ask for much more luck than that." Her voice was as pure in this realm as it had been when she had arrived from another; she was nothing but western Arkansas. That was the difference.

Melmer
Dunmore

Norris

IV

There weren't many people in Charleston during the Depression. There aren't many more now, either. The 1930 census enumerated 853, all white because Niggertown was three miles away and surrounding Confederate Musterground Park. The 1970 census counted exactly five hundred more, but Niggertown was gone. One of our more substantial citizens, a blacksmith with wicked armpits and an abiding hatred of Henry

Ford, used to insist that there were really twenty-five thousand people in Charleston. He stayed with that dream so long that he was finally removed and the demise of the blacksmithing business was left to a man named Wilhite, who decided to specialize in the new whim, Model A Fords, and he too might have faded had not he been rescued by somebody else. Precisely two somebody elses, one of whom was Melmer Dunmore.

Melmer was a local boy. His mother, a tiny woman, was blown away by the winter wind of 1929. His father took up travel and never came home again. Melmer had a sister who raised him; she was an old maid who died, somehow or other, during the winter of 1934. They were the ugliest people I have ever seen. The eighty-five-pound mother was colored. Blue. The father was ordinary in everything but neck and head. The neck was huge, massive, but the head was small, and in a poor light he looked as if he had no head at all but had, instead, a face painted on the front side of his neck. If a tuft of kinky red hair hadn't grown on his skull, even the face might not have been found. The sister looked almost exactly like Melmer, nearly seven feet tall and so skinny she looked as if she might have been pulled through a keyhole.

Melmer was so tall he had to sit in the back seat of his Model A to drive it comfortably. He owned a filling station with a small repair garage attached, and when he wasn't busy he sat between the regular and ethyl pumps, his tiny buttocks perched on a cane-bottomed chair. He never smiled or grinned at anybody but Toy Hannah, the waitress at the Tourist Cafe. Melmer had the bad hots for Toy.

He was cold toward me. I don't really know why. Perhaps because he thought it was safe; my father was dead and my mother was crazy. When I passed his filling station, which I had to do to reach my shine stand at the barber shop, Melmer liked to holler funny sounds at me. I threw rocks at him.

He tried to run over me in his Model A too. He chased Topwater Mulligan completely off the Street and all the way around the courthouse before old Top came to his sense and ran inside. That wasn't wise on the part of Melmer; Top took up the regular habit of pissing in the gas tank of Melmer's Model A. It was early spring before Melmer caught on and installed a lock on the gas cap. But Top had his revenge.

Nobody ever knew it. Topwater didn't brag. Perhaps old Major Billings and I were the only people in Charleston who knew about Melmer's gas tank. I thought people should know, because Melmer was one of those people who had a place in the world and he should have been kept in it. But Will Bumpers was the only one who ever really did put Melmer in his place.

Mr. Bumpers was still around in 1938. He had his morals and he didn't monkey with them, nor did he allow anybody else that privilege. Doc Bollinger once told Mr. Bumpers that a bottle of beer in the middle of the afternoon would help his digestion. Another man would have sneaked the beer, but not Will Bumpers. While we gaped, Will Bumpers entered the Tourist Cafe and ordered beer. He tried it three times before he decided that alcohol was more painful than indigestion.

Mr. Bumpers was in the hardware business and most of his trade was rural. One of his customers was a Negro named Gillespie, a solemn little man who lived in Niggertown just outside the boundaries of the Confederate Musterground. Mr. Bumpers called him Mr. Gillespie, the first time I ever heard a white call a black mister.

Mr. Gillespie bought a tractor in 1938. It was the first one bought by a black in Franklin County. He put in a crop of two hundred acres, tomatoes, peas, beans, and okra. Mr. Bumpers signed the back-up papers.

It was Melmer Dunmore who foreclosed. Nobody ever knew why. He saw Mr. Gillespie walking down the Street one day, and from his cane-bottomed chair between regular and ethyl, Melmer bawled the length of the town, "Hey, nigger! You owe me ten dollars and eight cents in gas! Pay up!"

If any of the characters in the Old Testament had red hair and cold blue eyes, they might have looked the way Mr.

Bumpers did that day. When he heard that braying voice of Melmer Dunmore, Mr. Bumpers dipped into his cash register and from it removed his "wad," that little reserve of cash merchants tried to keep on hand during the Depression. He stepped onto the sidewalk and glared across the brilliance of sun that seemed to make the Street the hottest place in town. "How much does Mr. Gillespie owe you, Mr. Dunmore?"

Melmer recoiled slightly; nobody had ever heard so much grit in Mr. Bumpers's voice before. But Melmer had made his play, and we all placed a great deal of value on our unwillingness to back down. "Just what I said, ten dollars and eight cents!"

Mr. Bumpers counted out ten silver dollars and eight pennies, and then, one coin at a time, he threw them across the Street. I had never heard the massive ring of heavy silver on cement before. While we stared, somehow unwilling to laugh in the presence of a Bumpers temper we had never seen before, Melmer hopped about, gathering money. He had never looked so tall or so skinny or so uncoordinated.

"If I don't have a receipt before sundown, Mr. Dunmore, I'll come after it." And Mr. Bumpers disappeared into his hardware store.

That was the moment when I decided I could handle Melmer Dunmore.

Melmer drove up and down the Street almost a full hour after he had delivered the receipt, as if perhaps he wanted to show us that he hadn't been so scared of Will Bumpers. I made the mistake of crossing the Street because I wanted to take advantage of the good shade that falls on the porch of the hotel late in the afternoon. Melmer tried to run me down. If I hadn't stepped behind a telephone pole, he would have had me. That horn on his Model A, which played "Merrily We Roll Along," not only sounded silly, it sounded mean too. That afternoon he chased dogs, cats, even a couple of goats. A huge pasteboard box was blown onto the Street and Melmer flattened it. When that was done, satisfied, he went home.

I hated him. His habit of hiding his hands just a little *too* deep in the bib of his overalls. The thin, wet line of his mouth. The braying voice. The shattering jeer of his laughter. The bantering hostility of his shifting, shiftless eyes that were so gray they almost matched those of Pistol Pete Murchison. But I could have forgiven him all those things had not he hated me even more than I hated him. "Hey, boy, when'd them wheels in your maw's head commence getting rusty, anyhow?" I couldn't forgive him for that.

I thirsted first, then hungered after revenge. The summer was a long one, but that was how much time it took for me to figure out how I would handle Melmer. Seated on a limb high in one of the walnut trees on the courthouse lawn, I spent hours watching Melmer at his filling station. I could have spent that time more profitably at my shine stand. Old Topwater joined me there more often than not. That was almost like home to Top; he lived in a tree with Major Billings.

Melmer cruised up and down the Street every afternoon for a while after closing time. Indolent, magnificently bored, the engine on his Model A clucking, Melmer liked to grin at girls and spit when he passed somebody he could afford to hate. Sometimes he entertained himself by repeatedly bumping a pasteboard box the wind had blown onto the Street.

That was when I made up my mind. That was when I became inspired.

I climbed out of the walnut tree and, followed by Topwater, went to the bench in front of the Tourist Cafe. I waited there until Melmer got his fill of bumping the pasteboard box. It took a while. Elaborately casual, his left hand steering and his right hand draped over the top of the wheel, bathing his teeth with his tongue, spitting, Melmer stayed with the box until almost dark.

Then he went to the Tourist Cafe. His hands were a little too busy inside the bib of his overalls and his thin little mouth had never looked so wet or uneven as he hauled himself heavily onto a stool and nodded ponderously at Toy. "I'll have my usual, Toy." And he sighed heavily.

Toy didn't move an inch. "I don't remember that you've ever been in this eating establishment before, boy.''

Lofty with aplomb, Melmer put her in her place. ''Bowl of chili and a Dr. Pepper. I had me a Dr. Pepper at ten, two, and four, but I like me a cold Dr. Pepper with my chili.''

Toy snapped her fingers. ''Now I remember you!''

''Figgered you would.'' I guess Melmer really did figure she would.

''You're Mickey Rooney!'' And before Melmer could say another word, she hurried on to get his chili and Dr. Pepper. When she placed the order before him, she asked politely, ''Mr. Rooney, would you like one cracker or two with your chili?''

Melmer grabbed the crackers and went to work. Perhaps he put up with Toy because, in a way, she was probably as miserable as he was, but Toy never tried to hurt anybody but Melmer. Indeed, Colonel Pettibone had been heard to remark that Toy was more of a lady than some of Charleston's real ladies. But she never missed an opportunity to slight Melmer.

Melmer tried to backtrack by flirting. He liked to flirt. He practiced every chance he got. Mostly it was rattling the change in his pocket or pretending to count the green in his billfold or driving by with his Model A playing "Merrily We Roll Along," but it was the kind of flirting Melmer liked and he was good at it. "Toy . . ." And he waited until she was standing before him.

"Yes, Mr. Rooney? Another Dr. Pepper?"

"Why don't you and me just take us a ride up to Fort Smith and see us a pitcher show?"

Toy couldn't believe it. *"Me?"*

"Ain't nobody else but."

"An old country girl like me on a date with Mickey Rooney! Gosh!"

Frequently enough, she went. Some of us attempted to find out what kind of date Melmer was, what kind of conversation he produced, but Toy merely shrugged. She didn't believe in trading secrets, so she never told us.

But tonight, while he ate his chili and drank his Dr. Pepper, there was

64

something — my heart — beating against the terror of Melmer Dunmore, so I couldn't help myself. I had to jeer, "Aren't you a little tall to be going out with Mickey Rooney, Toy?"

Before I saw it coming, one of those long Dunmore arms raked across the counter and the back of his hand caught me at the side of my head. I tumbled and sprawled. That, the poet says, was the last straw.

There was a design in my revenge, but I needed help and I had only two friends, Windy Spears and Top. Windy never heard it. Top disappeared in Fort Smith for a couple of weeks, and when he got back he had two gold teeth in the front of his mouth, engraved T.M. He spent a week walking around town, grinning at anybody who happened along; it took that long for me to calm him down enough to explain my plan.

Topwater liked it. Another three days passed before we found the pasteboard box we wanted. It was big, almost square, five feet in all directions. One of those fancy Philco radios had been shipped to

Bumpers's hardware in it.

A week later we found the rock we wanted. We spent the nights of that week in a tree across the street from Toy's house. (Her house was less than a block from my own and I could occasionally hurry home to see that my mother had taken her medicine.)

From that tree, we could watch Melmer as he cruised past. The Cafe closed at eight, and even if he didn't always have a date with her, Melmer did like to drive slowly by Toy's house and play "Merrily We Roll Along" for her. One night toward the end of the week, we placed a pasteboard box in front of her house. It was a test. He knocked it almost a half-block with the first blow.

We found the rock we wanted. It was lying in a field not far from the bridge over Doctors Ford Creek. It was a beautiful thing, that rock, lichen-encrusted on three sides, moss-covered on the fourth. It measured five feet by four and a half. Perfect.

"But one thing's wrong, Top."

"What's that?"

"How you figger we'll ever get this rock to town?"

"I'll be right back." Topwater took some time; it was after sundown when I saw him again. He was driving a truck. "This'll do it."

"Isn't that J. O. Cone's truck?"

"Nobody else's but."

"What'd Mr. Cone have to say?"

"Nothing. He don't know I got it."

Even if the truck was equipped with a winch, it was almost 8:30 when we got the rock to town. We dumped it in front of Toy's house and Top hurried away to return Mr. Cone's truck. He was back in ten minutes.

There was no hurry. Perched in our tree, we waited. But there was no sight or sound of Melmer Dunmore. At 9:30, usually her bedtime, something prompted Toy to wonder about the presence of a pasteboard box in front of her house, and of course she had seen us in the tree. Toy had kept possession of those instincts that prompt country people to look into trees when they can't find an answer on the ground. Anyhow, "What you two fools doing up there?"

There was nothing to do but explain. It took some time. Toy punched at the pasteboard box and, sure enough, there was an enormous rock inside. "Gaw-doe-motty," Toy breathed. She pursed her lips and shook her head several times before she made up her mind. "Y'all'd better get inside."

Toy's was a one-room house. Living room, dining room, kitchen, bedroom. There was a privy a few steps away. Toy turned out her kerosene lamp because it generated heat not needed on a hot summer night and because she didn't want Melmer to know she had company and was staying up late.

"How old you, Top?"

"Same age boy there is."

"You look fifty."

"Cain't help that."

Just to show Toy that we were men of the world, I pinched one of those great bundles we called titties. She slapped me so hard my ears rang for something like a month of Sundays, but that was all right: she didn't really resent what I had done.

When I tried it again, I merely got my cowlick ruffled. If I hadn't been intent upon revenge, I might have had my first Experience that night.

Topwater was getting sleepy. "Wonder where old Melmer's at?"

Toy was elaborately confident. "He'll come by."

" 'Spect so?"

"He'll come by."

I ran home to give my mother her ten o'clock medicine, and I was hurrying back to Toy's house when I heard that crazy horn playing "Merrily We Roll Along." I scurried into the back door just in time to see him drive past.

"He missed it," I said.

But before I could leave, Toy took my hand. "Just set a spell. He'll come back by."

Topwater was getting a little itchy. "Hope so. We've been to some trouble."

"He'll come back by," Toy said. She had never sounded so confident. "He taken his sister to a Singing Convention in Greenwood tonight. He'll come back by."

"Hope so," I said.

"Even when he's been to a Singing Convention, he always comes by twice."

Melmer did drive by again. Sure enough, the presence of that pasteboard box was more than he could bear. He plowed into it, his horn beginning the tune, and he was prepared to knock it a full block. There was a hell of a racket. It was a curious combination of *klang* and *klunk*. Immediately following that sound was another one, entirely familiar. Melmer bellered.

It wasn't a holler. Nor was it a howl. It was a true-toned beller.

Toy sat upright and listened. "Hoddamnit, you two boys've hurt that damn fool." Then she raised her voice. *"Melmer?"*

Melmer wasn't hurt. Not really. But his Model A was a wreck and, sitting there in the silver summer moonlight, he needed intensive spiritual care. "Goddamnit, Toy, I need you bad and I need you right now, *hear?"* His voice was heard as far away as Colonel Pettibone's house, three blocks away.

Getting out of her little bitty house was

something Toy managed with some dispatch. She knocked me flat and she knocked old Top completely across the room, but nothing slowed her down. *"I'm acoming, Melmer boy!"*

They're grandparents now. The youngest daughter of Toy and Melmer is the only one on either side of the family to finish high school and then she enrolled at Arkansas Tech. When she came to sign up for Freshman English, she told me her mother had specified that she enroll in one of my two sections.

"Dunmore?" I said. "Melmer and Toy's daughter, huh?"

"Yes sir." The girl looked like neither of her parents. She was plump and healthy, and her eyes were clear; she could have been almost any mid-South eighteen-year-old. And then she giggled; it was a kind of a happy gurgle. "Now ain't you ashamed of what you done to my daddy's car?"

Colonel
Pettibone

norris

V

There were several old men in and around
Charleston who stoutly insisted upon
being called colonel, but Colonel
Pettibone was the only real one we had in
residence. We had a major, old Major
Billings, Topwater Mulligan's friend, and
a couple of captains, not to mention the
hordes of sergeants and such, but Colonel
Pettibone was the only real colonel.
Windy Spears had a congenital distaste
for Civil War veterans, because, in their

days of glory, a few of them had been even more accomplished liars than Windy. "They're liars and the truth ain't in 'em. If all them lies were true, the White House'd been in Richmond, Virginia, right now."

Windy and I had become close enough that I could tease him. "You're whistling when you ought to be singing, Windy."

Windy grinned at me, easily willing to share his guilt with a friend. "Oh, I'm a liar and the truth ain't in me, but them Confederate boys is all over the place, and I got my trade to protect."

Windy was right; those old fellows were all over the place. They didn't outnumber veterans of the World's War if they were counted in one way, but counted as combat veterans, they outnumbered the younger men to an almost shabby degree. Windy, for instance, had never heard a shot fired in anger.

Colonel Pettibone had. He enlisted as a private, but he was a lieutenant at First Manassas, a captain at Second Manassas, a major at Seven Days, and when Appomattox came, he was standing

73

before his own regiment, a colonel in command of seven teenage boys and one old man.

"Yeah, the Colonel's a hero, all right." Windy might have sounded reluctant had not there been something essential to his taste of the truth when he added, "The ones that've saw a fight don't talk much." That was Windy's way of saying he was Charleston's crack liar. "Ain't Colonel Pettibone in the history books?"

"Yes sir," I said. *"Battles and Leaders of the Civil War."*

With profound understanding, Windy nodded. "The Colonel gets my salute long's these old legs'll hold me up and long's this old hand can touch my forehead." Then Windy popped to attention and showed me the way he would salute the Colonel the next time he saw him.

The Colonel was amused, but there was no contempt in his amusement. If Windy wanted to suddenly assume a weakness of the hams, thus causing him to stagger melodramatically as he heisted himself to his feet when the Colonel appeared, that was all right with the Colonel. Chipper, his own eleven wounds long ago forgotten, the Colonel waved that gentlemanly decoration called a walking cane, pointed it flippantly up to acknowledge the salute, and then was on his way to attend to those dozen-odd rental houses and that thousand-odd acres of land he owned in and around Charleston. He was past ninety-five, almost a hundred, and he walked with a dapper cheer that made Windy — and even me — look like an old man.

Every Monday afternoon he came to me for a shine. He wore boots because he rode a horse; he never learned to drive a car. He wanted his boots blackened. He didn't want them shined. A thick application of black paste and a painting of blacking; that's what the Colonel wanted. A shine during the Depression cost a nickel, but the Colonel slyly unrolled his bullcod purse and fetched up a dime. He placed the dime in my hand as if the two of us were sole proprietors of the most magnificent conspiracy since the night he had caught me adding the words

"Under the Covers" after the title of every hymn in the Methodist Hymnal. That dime was placed deep in my palm, and then, with a nod to Luke Wingate and Red Spears, the custodians of hair in the barber shop, the Colonel was gone.

Windy appeared immediately. "How much'd he give you this time, boy?"

"Dime. But, Windy . . ."

"What?"

"He always acts like he'd rather me not tell."

Windy was immediately grateful for being allowed to participate in the conspiracy. "Then let's just not tell nobody, all right?"

"Yes sir, I guess so."

"That's a boy!" Windy peered furtively at the two barbers, then he whispered broadly. Because of that minor injury caused by the phosgene during the World's War, his whisper was easier to hear than his speaking voice. "If I ever catch you showing anything but respect for the Colonel, I'll turn you over my knee and I'll give you a case of the hotseats you'll not soon forget."

"Yes sir."

But I really didn't understand Windy's respect and admiration for the Colonel until, finally, the Colonel began to show his age. It seemed to happen all at once. During the summer of 1938, of course, because there were something like forty-three days when the temperature climbed above a hundred degrees. The Methodists were still holding revivals then, although they didn't take them as seriously as the Baptists, say, and that was when, abruptly, we all took notice of the decline of Colonel Pettibone.

Windy was a Baptist. But he believed in revivals. Or perhaps he went to the Methodist revival for the same reason that the rest of us did: the picture show was open only two nights a week and the revival was the only thing in town. With his sturdy little wife and his parade of children, Windy entered the Methodist sanctuary as if he were visiting dignitary. He and each of his brood dropped a penny into the pieplate when it was held hopefully under his nose.

The Colonel arrived during the singing

of the second hymn. The Methodists in Charleston weren't singers, not real ones. Indeed, some Methodist men considered the singing to be that portion of the service reserved for women, so they stood erect, frowning slightly, only occasionally murmuring a few words they remembered from a distant summer in that Summer Singing School Spread Benefield conducted over at the Baptist Church. Will Bumpers, a baritone, and Luke Smith, a tenor, sang along when they could remember the words. And so did Colonel Pettibone, although he did occasionally consult a hymnal. But among the men in this Methodist sanctuary only Windy Spears, a top tenor, put any vitality into the singing. His voice sailed effortlessly over and above the entire congregation.

During that revival, an ordeal that somehow lasted three weeks, Windy and his family sat immediately behind the Colonel.

I wasn't a regular churchgoer, and certainly I wasn't a devotee of revivals, Methodist or Baptist, but during the summer, when my mother was asleep with her medicine, there was nothing else to do. I was the one who noticed that Colonel Pettibone was losing his grip.

He entered briskly enough that night, and he bowed with a peculiarly archaic eloquence toward Windy's sturdy wife, shook Windy's hand. He even took time to gravely shake my hand too. But he was no more than seated when he sighed. Nobody had ever heard the Colonel sigh before. I fidgeted slightly, but by that time the third hymn had begun.

The Colonel didn't really go to sleep until the sermon began. The preacher, one of those characters who appear in lonely towns and then disappear without taking any of the loneliness with them, was preaching on the wages of sin. Somewhere on the back pews were three, perhaps even four, Onion Creek rowdies, and when they came to town, they sought out the brightest lights. Tonight the lights were those in the First Methodist Episcopal Church.

When the Colonel fell asleep, his head didn't drop. He was that gem among

Americans: almost a hundred years old, and he could attend any meeting and, head erect, sleep through the most profound, the most foolish of talks.

But he had reached the age when he couldn't keep his mouth closed. The chin dropped. After a few moments the Colonel developed a mild case of hiccoughs. And he snored. It went something like *hic-snort-burrr*. Those rowdies from Onion Creek snickered a couple of times, but when Mr. Bumpers glared at them, they kept their peace.

Then the preacher, aware that even the pastor, Brother King, was nodding in his pew, decided that volume would recapture attention he had not honorably won — not during this revival at least — and suddenly elected to shout, *"Wages of sin!"* Entirely out of context.

The Colonel was jolted. He hiccoughed, then he snorted, then his dentures fell. With a crisp, widely audible *click*. That click sounded much the same way a sword might have sounded when it was whipped out of its scabbard during that moment that the Colonel ordered the last regimental cavalry charge of the Civil War. There was a stir in the congregation, and even that stranger, the revivalist, glanced toward the Colonel.

But it was the Onion Creek rowdies who undid it. They howled — *"Waaa!"* — so loudly that it was heard outside. Brother King, the pastor, bolted to his feet and, old as he was, seemed prepared to do battle, but there was nothing but silence in that sanctuary now.

Windy was silent too, but he wasn't inactive. He rose from his pew, patted both the Colonel and Brother King on their shoulders, and then, with a kind of firm nod toward his wife and children, he stepped briskly to that rear tier of pews. He rudely gestured the rowdies outside.

I didn't witness the altercation. Somehow or other, it wouldn't have been right for me, young as I was, to have bolted outside to help a man three times my age. The preacher decided against his sermon, and instead we sang a hymn, "Are Ye Able?"

We sang all of it; there was no avoiding the third verse. But that wasn't enough. It took Windy fifteen minutes to perform his chore. When he reentered the sanctuary, he was breathing so heavily I thought he might die. His shirt was shredded and he had a nosebleed. Behind him, peering as if they were unable to understand what had struck them, the Onion Creek rowdies filed carefully back into the sanctuary and sat down.

There was a lot of talk about it. For a man drawing a disability pension, Windy sure had a lot of energy. He did an excellent job with those rowdies.

The Colonel drew up his will the next day and died a few days later. The will stipulated that Windy Spears would be in command of those ex-soldiers who stood prepared to bury any man who had put on a uniform in behalf of his country. The will left the thoroughly blackened boots to me. I was also designated official bugler because I played cornet in the band. I played Taps over the Colonel's grave and another cornet player played Echo in those trees that used to stand at the top of the hill where Nixon Graveyard is. That was before the dry spell of 1954 killed the trees and drove the songbirds away.

Norris

Pistol Pete

VI

Pistol Pete was his real name. His father, a toothless old man with rubbery skin and an obscene quality in his voice that could have made the Lord's Prayer sound like a dirty joke, said he named his youngest son Pistol Pete because an itinerant gunsmith was probably the boy's father.

Pete had but one job in his entire life. He was first elected constable of Onion Creek Township in 1911. It was a position he'd won easily, not because he was a good peace officer, but because it was said the township didn't need a constable, and if Pete got the job there wouldn't be one. Rural life was duller then than now, and we were obliged to manufacture our own clowns rather than depend on the Gem Theater, which was open only two nights a week.

Pete couldn't read and he couldn't write. When he occasionally received mail, he brought it to my shine stand and I read it aloud to him several times. Judge Wilkins, he who clung to the pretense that he had served as a major in the First Arkansas Mounted Rifles so long that, as he lay dying, he called for General Churchill — it was the Judge who drilled Pete until he could parrot the speeches necessary for the serving of legal papers to those obliged to appear in the Judge's court. When I sometimes asked Pete why he never learned to read and write, he had an easy and entirely logical answer. "Ain't no use. My family all lives at home, so I don't write no letters. When I get mail, you read it to me. Besides, Mr. Pennypacker" — our superintendent of schools at the time — "he'd have a fit if I come walking up there and said I want in books."

It would seem that Pete was another one of those middle-aged men who shuffled through the Depression, but he did prompt a second glance. His skin was dark, Indian dark — but that gunsmith hadn't been an Indian — and his eyes were gray, almost dirty white, but his mother had brown eyes and his father had had green. His mouth was small but his lips were exceptionally full, and when he spoke or laughed or yodeled, his mouth looked like a small doughnut. He seemed to be bald and without eyebrows, but that second glance revealed that his hair was exactly the color of his skin.

He had a high voice, but it wasn't girlish. It was raspy, but he wasn't a bad gospel tenor; indeed, had it not been for the presence of Windy Spears, Pete might have made his mark as top tenor in the quartet. He could yell the length of the Street, and if no trucks were passing through town, he could be easily heard at the ice house, a full two blocks away.

He found and wore a bowler, one of those potlike things, and it was just a mite too large, so that it rested on his ears, which, as the years passed, flopped from having borne the weight of the hat. He didn't wear overalls, as most middle-aged men did during the Depression; he wore, instead, a pair of hickory pants, those light canvas things that looked faintly like butternut. His shirt was pink now but it had once been red. He wore no underwear. At winter he had found and now wore an overcoat that struck his heels. Because Pete was above average height, the original owner of that coat must have been a giant.

That was Pistol Pete Murchison. During the forty years he served as constable he never once made an arrest. He carried a pistol, of course — a long, rather ugly thing which he used to dispose of aging cats and diseased dogs. But the pistol wasn't really a weapon of the law.

Pete once found himself assigned to the task of transporting a patient to the Hospital for the Criminally Insane near Traskwood in Saline County. He talked about the trip — it required two days because the roads were poor and his Model T was unwilling — for months, and finally, perhaps because he trusted me or perhaps he just couldn't stop talking, he let it slip that the guards at the hospital confused him with the patient, and only the possession of the pistol saved Pete from a fate he wasn't willing to imagine.

When the bank was robbed, Pete hid his pistol, jumped in his Model T and headed east. The robbers headed west. He was teased about that, but he didn't seem to mind. "Hell! Hang around and get shot! Let Windy and that engineer catch the bank robber; I'll mind my own business."

It was cowardice, perhaps, that gave him so much entertainment value. He was even scared of the Judge, whose aristocratic pretenses were also a form of entertainment to us, and when the Judge scolded Pete, he felt an obligation to prove to us that, even scolded, he wasn't to be taken seriously. On those occasions he crawled into his Model T and, cranking the siren, drove up and back the length of the Street, cackling all sorts of things likely to prove he was foolish. "Lo and behold, they went to the top of the mountain and et collards and black-eyed peas." Or "Shall we gather at the river; I need a good bath bad."

Because we were rural people and therefore obliging, we didn't laugh behind his back. He was silly and funny because that was what he wanted to be; he might be assigned a dangerous duty if he was taken seriously. He wanted to be a clown, and indeed, with the hickory and the shirt and the bowler and the overcoat and the pistol, he did dress something like a circus clown. And the siren, of course; he stole that from the fire truck.

It was the pistol and the siren that almost got Pete killed.

It was a hot afternoon, one of those thousands which bedeviled Charleston and will continue to do so. The crops were laid by and the farmers had nothing to do but loaf. The quartet was singing in Spreading Adder Benefield's shop, and there was a domino game at the pool hall and some checkers at the ice house, but mostly the Street was silent. Two cars arrived, one from the east and one from the west, and they met at the hotel. One of the cars was a black '33 V-8 and the other one was a brown knee-action Chevrolet. They prompted no attention at all; I thought they were WPA officials on a field trip.

People remembered the afternoon, and for years we carefully fabricated lies about our activities. J. O. Cone, one of our two grocers, was taking a nap on the counter by the cash box. Dock Frye, the proprietor of the Tourist Cafe, was treating himself to the delicacies of his life, Limburger and Falstaff. Will Bumpers was preparing his Sunday school lesson. Luke Wingate and Red Spears were asleep in their barber chairs and I was lazily watching the progress of five dogs in pursuit of a female in heat. Everybody else made up a lie and stuck to it.

All of us heard Pete's siren, and it occurred to all of us that it was too hot for Pete to be putting that much energy into cracking the fool thing. I was the only one who stepped to the Street to see where Pete was going. He stopped at the hotel.

The siren had a stop button on it, but Pete liked to hear the thing's moan decrease to silence. Besides, it added importance to his entrance into the lobby of the hotel. So it was still moaning when Pete briskly mounted the wooden steps of the hotel and stomped across that vine-bemused porch. He had a piece of paper in his hand; he was on official business.

He walked right past the strangers and paid them hardly any attention at all. The hotel, long since burned to the ground because the connection to its insurance policy overheated, was so bevined and latticed that there was a deep green shade on its porch that almost obscured the entrance. So Pete, briskly slapping his thigh with the papers, nodded curtly at what he thought was a group of Falstaff drinkers, and didn't know until he was quite old that he had passed, fully armed, within twenty paces of them.

Nothing prompted Pete to imagine anything was amiss. He paused in the lobby a moment to accustom his eyes to the gloom. It was one of those old-fashioned hotels — it had once been a real

one before the mines stopped working —
and there was a lot of dark paneling
around, so Pete was slow in discovering
that Old Cat wasn't around. Instead, there
was a stranger behind the desk.

"Who you, boy?" Twenty years passed
before Pete admitted that he had also
said, "You sure got a funny-looking pair
of eyes on you."

The stranger's eyes were almost
exactly like Pete's. Perhaps the malice in
them made the only difference, because
they were looking at Pete over the barrels
of a shotgun. Pete later recalled that the
man's voice didn't have a whole lot of
tune to it. "Let me tell you what I aim for
you to do, brother."

"What's that?" Pete was beginning to
think he was being confused with a patient
again.

"You aim to stick your right hand
straight up in the air and then you aim to
use your left hand to undo the buckle on
that pistol belt."

Then Pete caught on. "Aw hell, boy, I
ain't no holdup man! I'm just Pistol
Pete!"

"That's fine. Now with your left hand —"

"Aw hell." Pete slapped the papers on the desk in front of the man. "You tell Old Cat when she comes back she's gonna be in court come a week from this Thursday." Irritably enough, Pete shoved the shotgun aside. "Hell, boy, I done told you once, I ain't no holdup man!"

Pete whistled as he left the lobby. He might have seen them on the porch, but the sun had dropped below the eaves of the courthouse, which permitted a single sunray to penetrate the green silence of the porch, and it shone directly into Pete's eyes.

He spoke cheerfully to the people on the porch. "How y'all?" But he couldn't see them; he didn't know that two men and a woman all had pistols pointed at him. He mounted his Model T and, cracking the siren, made his way back to the courthouse.

The stranger with the shotgun was never identified, but within minutes after the people left the hotel and Old Cat managed to free herself we knew who the two men and the woman were. Pete, like the cuckolded husband, was the last to know.

Those people had been dead twenty years and Pete was approaching his senility when I visited Charleston one afternoon and told him who they were: Clyde Barrow, Bonnie Parker, and Pretty Boy Floyd, meeting in Charleston to make an agreement on territory. Pete fainted dead away, but when he recovered, he spent the remainder of his days amused by what had almost happened to him.

Mr. Pennypacker

Norris

VII

He came to Charleston early in the Depression, taught history a couple of years, found himself appointed superintendent of schools, and then, when he was defeated, he disappeared. J. M. Pennypacker.

Mr. Pennypacker was a natural challenge to those two-hundred-odd of us who resented all classes but Miss Doll's, with that tedium of pencils and ennui of tablets and cold lunches carried to school in empty lard buckets, the lids of which were perforated by stabbings of a butcher knife so that air circulation would help prevent the spoiling of cold biscuits and side meat. Of course we would have hated him anyhow; he was one of those little men impressed with small authority. He terrorized his teachers, all but Miss Doll, who was afraid of nothing and of nobody. He was hard on us students too; only Topwater Mulligan, who shuffled through the Depression unassailed by anybody, didn't resent the pressure Mr. Pennypacker kept on the students. To Top, the Depression was merely a series of morning fogs in the valleys, and Mr. Pennypacker was simply another fog.

He was a quick little man who took short steps and pecked as he walked. He reddened easily. His eyes were dirty gray, but when he lost his temper, which was often enough, his eyes actually changed color because his pupils dilated. There was a curious anomaly concerning his fingernails too; they curled over the tips of his fingers. He carried a small grayhandled penknife, and as he pecked through his teaching and administrative day, he spent a lot of quick time prying real and imaginary bits of dirt from beneath those fingernails.

He taught a course, even after he became superintendent, called P.I.A.D., Problems in American Democracy. The course is still taught under the title Americanism vs. Communism, but during the Depression it wasn't thought subversive to confess that our democracy could have problems.

I thought Mr. Pennypacker was one of those problems. Topwater agreed on the basis of our friendship, but, enthroned in Mr. Pennypacker's classroom, his great, sad face not at all aglow with the majesty of the learning situation, it was obvious that Top didn't really care one way or another.

For some reason, that face of Top's bothered Mr. Pennypacker, perhaps because it showed so little. So at least once a day Mr. Pennypacker called on Top to recite. That caused Top to have to prepare his lessons, which he did by sort of hanging around me while I did mine.

It all began innocently enough. "Topwater, tell me what — Is Topwater your real name?"

Something might have stirred in that face. "It is to me." Top's real name was James Marvin Wesley Sidebottom Mulligan, and he was sensitive about it.

Perhaps Mr. Pennypacker also saw something stir in that face, or perhaps he wanted to hurry on with the lesson; he dropped Top's real name. "Now, Topwater, tell me how to spell *bolshevism.*"

Top's manner was deliberate but he didn't hesitate. "B-U-L-L-S-H-I-T-I-S-M."

That's how it began.

Mr. Pennypacker was so dumbfounded that for seconds he didn't even turn red, and even so he was unable to remember for hours that he should have hauled Top to his office, bent him over the tardy desk, and paddled him. That would have happened ordinarily; the solid whack of the paddle smashing against skinny buttocks was an almost daily sound at CHS.

Top was immediately a hero. Windy Spears, Scrooge Wilkins, Brother King, and Mr. Slim all made it a point to greet Top with a cheerful salute when he made his way to the Creasant Drug Store, where Top swept out afternoons after school. Top handled it easily enough.

But he didn't reckon with Mr. J. M. Pennypacker. Almost three weeks passed before Mr. Pennypacker caused his path to cross Top's. It happened not in P.I.A.D. but in the hall between classes. Top's locker was near Miss Doll's room, and he sometimes sort of drifted by her door in hopes that she would speak to him. Of course, Top at full speed still looked like he might be loitering, which wasn't allowed in the halls, so if he was drifting, he looked like he might be up to something. Before Top could make up his mind about what was going on, he was hustled into the office, bent over the tardy desk, and paddled.

Mr. Pennypacker usually made it a practice to announce the quantity of punishment in as calm a voice as he could produce, but he lusted after that paddle so passionately that he couldn't stay calm; he panted. And he always lost control. He promised Top five licks, but he was so stimulated that he delivered thirteen before, crying wildly, Topwater broke and ran.

Mr. Pennypacker chased him almost to the Tiger's Den, a block away, before he stopped. Then, his face brilliant and his breath wild, he made threatening gestures with the paddle. He stood there for perhaps five minutes — until Top disappeared toward that tree where he and old Major Billings lived — and then Mr. Pennypacker returned to his office. He did no more work that day, and when school was out at 4:15 he got into his car and drove away.

In that car, a 1927 Chevrolet with a cloth top and wooden bows, Mr. Pennypacker drove past Top's tree a half-dozen times before he drove on home. His wife, a fleshy woman with a bucolic whine that rose effortlessly above the roofs of Charleston, told her neighbors she didn't understand her husband at all. "Every time he gives one them boys a paddling, he comes home and just plain wears me down to nothing. Won't even give me time to get his eats on the table."

Windy Spears was at the hotel telling Old Cat about the time he had fired the last shot of the World's War when I found him. After I finished telling him about the paddling, he sat there a long time, the longest I had ever seen him silent, so long that even Old Cat looked slightly alarmed.

"Thirteen licks, you say, boy?"

"Yes sir. Easy to count; we could hear it all over the building."

"And Top cried, you say?"

"Yes sir."

There was another long silence; then Windy said, "You come on with me, boy."

We went to Top's house. Moving rather stiffly, he was preparing supper for himself and his house guest, Major Billings. The wind was swaying the tree and that made Windy slightly nervous, but he wasn't to be detoured. "Let me take a look at that bottom of yours, Top."

Top was going to have to sleep on his stomach for a few days.

Windy was late getting home that night. He walked with me and visited with my mother awhile. He was one of the few people in Charleston who made a serious effort to talk to her. Her mind, misty at best, seemed clearer in Windy's presence than at any other time. And while he was talking to Momma, it came to him.

"Just like the word of the Lord!" That's the way Windy put it for days. "Just *like* it!"

So everybody in town knew what Windy planned to do, but, proof of the sort of people we were, Mr. Pennypacker never heard a word of it. Topwater was opposed to the plan, but Windy wouldn't listen. He even prevailed upon Top to steal a fifty-foot length of steel cable and two heavy-duty clamps from the Bumpers Hardware and Funeral Home Company. But a month, and then another month, passed and nothing happened.

"What's the holdup?"

"If things ain't just right, they're plumb wrong." Windy was so intent on the project that he hadn't told a really good lie in almost seven weeks. He was even omitting colorful detail from lies he had rehearsed as early as 1920. "It's gonna be right or we won't do it."

So another month and it was spring. Public schools still had the spring rally in those days. A couple of weeks before the summer vacation, every school in Franklin County sent its champion spellers, its best "expression" students, those memory experts who could recite "The Declaration of Independence," its musicians — any student with a talent of any sort, real or imagined — all to the county seat, Charleston, where they were paired against students from all over the county. School buses, not yellow then, clogged the Street and parked all over the school grounds.

Mr. Pennypacker didn't park his Chevrolet in the right place, but he was so distracted by the pressures of the day — he was in a rage for seven solid hours — that he didn't notice when I moved it. Its rear bumper was square against the gas meter by the study hall door. One of the smaller boys was shoved through a ventilation opening, pulling the cable and one of the clamps behind him.

Topwater still didn't approve, but he was reciting a poem in one of the contests and he couldn't hang around to argue with us. (The judges liked his rendition of "The Boy Stood on the Burning Deck" because, although there was warmth in his voice, his face hardly moved at all.)

Topwater even won a medal, third place, as he always had, but when his name was called at Assembly at the end of the day, it would have been thought he had won the sweepstakes medal; he was cheered wildly. Windy was master of ceremonies, and he had a good time with the presentation.

"Ladies and gentlemen, I don't remember that I've been as proud in my life, except for that third Croix de Guerre I won, maybe. Topwater Mulligan has been one of my favorites since I first marched back from Over There. And now he has won a medal, even after the superintendent beat him almost to death last winter."

That was the magic moment. Mr. Pennypacker, his face seething, jumped up from his place among the privileged and opened his mouth to say something terrible, but Scrooge Wilkins jerked his sleeve, and Mr. Pennypacker got a good enough hold on himself that he left without saying a word. Through the windows of the auditorium we could see him hurrying toward his car. He stopped once and shook his fist at us, but he didn't holler or carry on.

The Chevrolet started immediately. Mr. Pennypacker jerked it into gear. If his departure had been made for the purpose of impressing us with the forty horses of power the Chevrolet had, it would have been spectacular.

At the end of the cable, the car stopped. Well, some of it did. Clamped to the gas meter, it couldn't have gone much farther. The rear wheels, the drive shaft, and the transmission stopped dead cold, but the rest of the car traveled a few feet farther toward Highway 22. Mr. Pennypacker almost bit the steering wheel in two.

For almost a minute there was nothing but silence as we left the auditorium and gathered about the car. The first sound was that of soft crying. It came from Mr. Pennypacker. Topwater gently helped him from the car and sat him down on the running board. Mr. Pennypacker's lips were bloody.

Topwater looked up at Windy and said, "Go get Doc Bollinger."

Windy kind of fidgeted a moment before he said shortly, "I 'spect I'd better."

There were only two more weeks of school, and a truce, tacit but rigid, was effected; Mr. Pennypacker was left alone. At the meeting of the school board prior to graduation exercises, Mr. Pennypacker resigned. He gave no reason and the board didn't ask for one. As he walked home that afternoon — he couldn't afford to repair his car — most of us went out of our way to speak to him.

"Afternoon, Mr. Pennypacker."

By the time the fourth or fifth of us had spoken, he realized what we were trying to do, and perhaps for the first time in his life he drew himself up and somewhere found a kind of practical dignity that immediately became a part of the man's essentials. That night we dragged his car to the Pendergrass & Flanagan garage and went to work. Topwater was in charge. We were through with it by sunrise.

The car wasn't as good as new. No 1927 Chevrolet could sustain a blow like that and come back in perfect shape. But it was tight again, neat in the same way that model had always been, and its symbolism was functional.

There was no testimonial dinner when he left. As he drove out of town he stopped at the Conoco for gasoline, and within moments as many as a hundred of us had gathered around his car. All of us spoke to him — "Morning, Mr. Pennypacker" — in quiet voices, as if perhaps we didn't want to sound as if we were glad to see him go, and he answered, calling us by name. His wife, bewildered, didn't say a word.

Topwater was the last one to appear. Somehow that sad face of his cheered things up. Nick Monroe helped too; when Mr. Pennypacker hauled out his bullcod to pay for the gasoline, Nick wouldn't take a cent. There was some slow grinning and shuffling about, and if any of us had had the courage, we might have started a cheer.

It was Windy who made the farewell easy: he leaned into the Chevrolet and kissed Mrs. Pennypacker right on the mouth. "I been wanted to do that since the day I first laid eyes on you, Miz Pennypacker," Windy said loudly. We knew he was lying, but we were pleased too. "Bring your husband and call on us some o' these days."

Tears suddenly appeared in Mr. Pennypacker's eyes and he started the engine.

"Wait a minute!" Windy gestured toward me. "Boy, you look and make sure some fool didn't tie a cable on his car again."

And all of us, even Mrs. Pennypacker, laughed. As Mr. Pennypacker drove on to Highway 22 and away, we even cheered.

There's no telling where Mr. Pennypacker went. Some of us knew that he finally amounted to something; at any rate he had access to military records, because regularly, during the war, we received letters from him. The survivors of our dead received telegrams immediately following the one from the

108

Adjutant General. But none of us ever found out where Mr. Pennypacker went. Perhaps we didn't really need to know.

Scrooge

Norris

VIII

It was Windy Spears who called him Scrooge. His real name was Royal Wilkins, but Windy had a fine talent for hyperbole; Royal Wilkins was no Scrooge. But even if he was as generous a man as there was in Charleston, with the possible exception of Brother King, that's what we called him. Scrooge Wilkins.

Scrooge came to Charleston in 1932 when he married Bessie Grimes, the oldest of that squadron of Grimes daughters, a family which used to boast that they were kin to Miss Hettie McIntosh. Bessie Grimes Wilkins was a big woman, full at the breast and wide at the hip, and her voice had a certain quality that made her sound as if she might have been kin to Melmer Dunmore. She wasn't. She was the kind of big woman who would prompt Windy to say, "Them big old women'll pick 'em a quiet little man every time." Windy also noted that Bessie kept herself quiet and prissy in Scrooge's presence.

Scrooge was what Windy called him, quiet. His voice was hardly above a whisper, and although he did wear Friendly Fives with steep caps on the heels, he was quieter than anybody in town except Topwater Mulligan. Scrooge weighed about a hundred and thirty pounds. He wore spats, a gray twill suit, and a black satin vest. His eyes were blue, clear water blue, and they tended to water slightly. He looked slightly apologetic because he smiled nearly always.

Windy admired Scrooge because the man was so industrious. When he came to

Charleston he rented the building where the Old Triangle Shoppe had been before the Crash, and while most of us loafed and cursed, Scrooge brought men in to remodel the place. He wasn't the sort of man who volunteered information, and nobody in Charleston knew how to ask a direct question; thus we didn't know what kind of business he had in mind for the building.

When his sign was delivered, his secret was out: he was opening a restaurant. A cafe. For forty years now there had been two eating places in Charleston, the Tourist Cafe and the hotel. With business still going downhill after the Crash, it didn't seem reasonable that we could support another eating establishment. But when we saw the sign, we began to feel sorry for Scrooge's competition. "The Trucker's Cafe," it read.

It was our first neon sign. Coming over Schoolhouse Hill, it was the first — and about the only — thing seen of Charleston at night. It brightened up the Street, and Windy was so deeply moved that he composed a poem. "Good old

Charleston," it began. "I knowed you'd amount to something someday." We stopped grinning at Scrooge's spats and the suit and we stopped punching each other when Bessie lowered her voice in his presence.

Scrooge didn't want the place to become a beer joint, so he would sell it only when it was drunk with food. Our visiting hellraisers, the Onion Creek rowdies, all of whom liked to start a little trouble in town on a Saturday night, vowed they would clean out that cafe if they were refused beer, but Scrooge took care of them as easily as he did the others. "Beer, yes sir, gentlemen. And what would you like to eat with your beer?" The rowdies had never heard a voice that soft, and they had never been called gentlemen before either. They ordered what they called a "hamburglar sangwitch," and from that moment on they allowed no criticism of Scrooge within their earshot.

The cafe flourished. Even if Bessie was kind of bossy when she was obliged to work, it flourished. The food wasn't excellent. Arkansas had never had an excellent restaurant. But it was good. Instead of the standard plate lunch, Scrooge offered a choice of three, each named for the color of the plate on which it was served, just like they did in the cities. In season, Scrooge's vegetables came from the gardens of Mr. Slim, the Tomato Man, he who was uncomfortable in any conversation that strayed from vegetables.

Scrooge didn't get rich. There were no rich people in Charleston, and there probably aren't any now either. But Scrooge did prosper. He didn't hurt the Tourist Cafe, because a lot of beer was drunk there. Indeed, there were people in Franklin County who had eaten their first food away from home at the Tourist Cafe, and the experience had been such a heady one that they didn't trust themselves to go on to better things. The hotel prepared food only for its own guests, and Old Cat had been known to be quite rude to anybody who wanted to horn in on her family-style feeding system.

Scrooge's business was mostly

transient. Highway 22 was popular with truckers, because from Fort Smith to Russellville it was the straighter choice and its hills the more gentle. The truckers also liked to be called gentlemen. Gentlemen of the road, they wanted to be called. There were people during the Depression who romanticized Clyde Barrow and Bonnie Parker, so they had no trouble imagining a truck driver as a gentleman. Any cafe almost obscured by trucks was bound to be a good place to eat. The truckers themselves took their reputations so seriously that they bestowed their presence only on favorites, Scrooge Wilkins being one of those.

Windy wasn't a friend of Scrooge's, not really. I don't suppose Windy was actually close to anybody who couldn't read shaped notes, and Windy wasn't a drinking man either, so after his morning cup of coffee with Dock Frye at the Tourist Cafe he had no further use for that place during the day. Because he was on a pension, he could afford an occasional extravagance; thus he could afford a hamburger and a Dr. Pepper during the afternoons. A hamburger contained a quarter-pound of meat and enough of Mr. Slim's vegetables to constitute a balanced diet — and the whole thing was a nickel. The drink was another nickel. Scrooge liked vegetables, so he often enough joined Windy in eating huge cartwheels of tomato slices and slaw and lettuce and white onions and fried okra while they talked. So even if they weren't friends, Windy was fond of Scrooge.

"They ain't another man in town like 'im." Windy pondered a moment. "Or anywhere else in the world that I've met in my travels. If I'd been chored to find a gentleman and I had to look beyond Will Bumpers and Brother King, I'd pick Scrooge Wilkins."

Almost all of us felt the same way. A few people from one or another of the churches felt duty-bound to hate Scrooge because, after all, he did sell beer, but our Methodist preacher, Brother King, occasionally made it a point to have Sunday dinner with Scrooge, so as time inched along, Scrooge Wilkins became an important man in Charleston. He was

116

even put up for and was elected to the school board. He didn't rank with Will Bumpers or Brother King or Old Cat or Miss Hettie McIntosh, but Scrooge was a favorite.

Then one day he disappeared.

Bessie came to work and so the financial affairs of the Cafe were in safe hands, but nobody asked her any questions. Truckers continued to stop, but they didn't stay long. They couldn't stand Bessie's voice; it sounded as if somebody had dropped a handful of steelies in her transmission.

That lasted two weeks, then Scrooge reappeared. He stepped off the bus on Saturday afternoon and went into his cafe and, without so much as a nod to Bessie, went back to work. Bessie snuffed a few times, then she went home. We didn't crowd around Scrooge; we weren't that sort of people. But we did sort of mosey by, sidle up next to, and generally give him a study.

"Afternoon, Scrooge."

Scrooge politely returned each greeting.

"Wonder where it is that he's been?"

Windy murmured. Windy could wonder longer about that sort of thing than the rest of us would.

Most of us never knew where he went. Scrooge disappeared for two weeks just about twice a year, usually in the early spring and late fall. Windy, who had nothing else to do except maintain studies of our citizenry, somehow decided that Scrooge was going somewhere for his health, because he disappeared only when the mean temperature was below eighty and above sixty.

The Trucker's Cafe continued to prosper. Scrooge even bought a car. Not a new one. The '37 Fords were kind of a gothic design anyhow. He bought a '34 Ford, blue, with a white cloth top and wooden bows and a rumble seat too. It was forever flawlessly clean; it was the dream of all of us who didn't own cars. But Scrooge was dignified at the wheel. Bessie, who was usually busy being pregnant when it became obvious that they could afford children, was the one who loved that car. If she could have strutted while seated and with her lap occupied by three children, that's what she would have done when Scrooge drove his family down the street.

And finally, by 1938, we had learned to accept Scrooge's semiannual disappearances the same way we accepted Windy's lies, Brother King's sermons, Miss Hettie's beauty, and Spread Benefield's stomach. We had even learned to accept the Depression.

But for one reason or another, Windy didn't find acceptance all that easy. "Wonder where it is that he's been?" Windy was fascinated by the man: that saintly smile, that almost silent voice, those clothes, the gentle conversation. Windy had found a man of such infinite complication that he had to have the answer.

He might not have ever had it if the Veterans Administration hadn't wondered about those lungs of Windy's. By regulation, he was supposed to appear twice a year at a recognized Veterans Facility for examination, but because there was no arguing with the lungs of a gassed veteran, Windy hadn't been examined in something like ten years. The Veterans Administration ordered him to Little Rock.

It was an event. Windy's solid little wife and all those children would have made it an event even if nobody else had been interested. They gathered at the drugstore, where bus tickets were sold, and they moaned and wailed and caterwauled for a solid hour, as if perhaps Windy were going back to the trenches Over There again. Windy enjoyed the attention. He also stood to profit some seven dollars, because his wife had prepared a shoebox of eats and he could pocket his food allowance. Besides, he might pick up something that would add substantial detail to one of his weaker lies.

In Little Rock, a mecca almost as distant as, say, Dallas, Windy discovered the truth about Scrooge's disappearances. Windy was smart enough to admit that he was a country boy when he was in a town as much as twice the size of Charleston, so when he found himself lost in Little Rock, he knew exactly what to do. He placed himself at the mercy of somebody in the city. He needed to know what bus to take. "I'm just a country boy and I need help." The bus driver was a country boy and, indeed, had found his way into the city by just the same admission that Windy delivered, so he took Windy in tow. He didn't even charge him fare, another nickel Windy could pocket.

That was when Windy saw Scrooge. That beautiful little '34 Ford, the top down, the rumble seat open, polished to a glittering shine, was on Broadway. Scrooge himself was in the rumble seat. He had his arms folded before him and on his face was an expression of unassailable arrogance. He occasionally offered an imperial gesture, but not many, for in a voice as loud as brass, he was giving orders to a Negro driver, obviously hired for the occasion and also obviously amused by that silly drunk in the rumble seat.

Windy shared that secret with me for a reason that neither of us fully understood, and then he took it to his grave, and I shall take it to mine. We didn't even tell

Scrooge. The two men continued to meet for Mr. Slim's vegetables and soft lazy conversation in the Trucker's Cafe and they never mentioned either Scrooge's secret or Windy's knowledge of it.

When Windy was buried, during the drought of 1954, Scrooge, who was not a veteran so not a member of the honor guard from the Legion that buried Windy, stood surrounded by those children Bessie had produced for him. The entire family, all eleven of them, were dressed in black, a color they wore until the end of the year. And when somebody broke and hungry came to the cafe and asked for food, Scrooge let them have it in the name of Windy Spears. That was the way Scrooge lived.

Clodd
McCall

Morris

IX

His mother's maiden name was Clodd, and so he was named Clodd McCall. He was Charleston's certified brawler. Always whining as if somehow he had been imposed upon, Clodd started at least one fight a day.

There was a kind of whining flourish in Clodd's style. There were things he wanted and things he wanted to do, and when they didn't come by him rightfully he whined, started a fight, and soon enough had things in his hands. He had a puckered mouth and baggy cheeks, clear blue eyes, and a flat forehead that prompted strangers to wonder if he might be the village idiot. Truckers sometimes teased him in the Trucker's Cafe. He regularly beat all of them senseless.

We left him alone.

I was afraid of him but I didn't hate him. There was something in that defensive whine that caused him sometimes to sound almost pathetic. But when he decided he wanted my shine stand, that was something else. (Before I left for the University, I sold the shine stand to the son of the bank's president; thus one knows now that I didn't crumple before Clodd's offense.)

"How much you make shining shoes?"

"About two dollars a week."

That made me the richest boy in town. Perhaps Melmer Dunmore hated me because I was the crazy widder's son, but I was making money. Clodd didn't hate me for any such reason; his mother had been a Clodd. It was simple; Clodd couldn't get a job at the Gem Theater, where he felt his talents lay, so he wanted the next best job in town, mine. He offered me ten dollars for my stand.

I didn't imagine I would ever keep the stand; I wasn't a brawler. But in those days it wasn't unusual to believe in the principles of a profit from one's speculations, so I held out for fifty dollars.

The effort exhausted me. Clodd shadowed me, suddenly appeared from behind signs and beneath buildings and out of trees, and stood before me, his arms folded and his beady eyes bristling with hatred and self-indulgence. I took a different route home at night. I administered my mother's medicine in darkness in hopes Clodd would think I wasn't at home. I threw cherrybombs into the mule barn, where Clodd spent most of his sleeping hours. None of it made any difference; Clodd was determined to get my shine stand for ten dollars.

The proprietor of the barber shop, Luke Wingate, was a good barber but he really wasn't smart. However, his instincts preserved him; he never got mixed up in other people's troubles. "Don't tell me about it. One shine boy's good as the next. That shine stand's there to service my haircutting trade. I don't get a dime out of it, so if you give me trouble with Clodd McCall, I'll throw you and the shine stand both out the back door." That would have been impossible, because there was a ten-foot mound of hair beyond the back door, but Luke didn't need to explain any further.

I bought a water pistol and loaded it with Tabasco sauce. One hot shot of that put Clodd in bed for a couple of days, but when he was again up and around, he blacked both my eyes and broke my nose. When he went swimming, alone, at Berry Creek, I sneaked up and stole his clothes. I didn't see him for a couple of days and, soon enough, his parents had the law out looking for him. He came home safely enough; it seems that a naked boy, moving cross-country, must move carefully, thus slowly. For that he broke two of my ribs.

Topwater let me handle it until it became obvious that I didn't know what I was doing. "You ain't handling it right."

Topwater's voice had a kind of burr in it; it didn't sound like it belonged to his face at all. "What you need to do's fix old Clodd so he'll never want to cross you again."

I had masterminded the cooling of Melmer Dunmore; I had devised ways and means of putting Spread Benefield's Model T on top of the American State Bank; to my shame, I had something to do with the departure of Mr. Pennypacker; I had stolen Constable Jack Winters's pistol right out of his holster. Surely I could handle this.

I did.

Events conspired in my behalf. The Davis-Brunk Comedians was a tent show. During the Depression they came to Charleston every summer. They arrived on a Sunday morning and erected the tent, and the first show was on a Monday night. They staged a play every night of the week, and on a Saturday night there was a special. The hero was always named either John or Clarence and the heroine was usually called Jane. The heavy had a kind of an aristocratic name, Stewart or

Smedley. The comic was invariably named Toby. The plots were budding love. Even after the Gem Theater went into business, Davis-Brunk drew capacity crowds almost every night. There were reserved seats, cruelly uncomfortable things of wood and canvas that restricted circulation in the legs, and there was a regular admission bleachers we called the Chicken Roost.

Davis-Brunk had a serious problem. They called it *leakage*. After the tent began to fill and after it began to billow with the heat created by four hundred pairs of armpits, slipping under the fly wasn't so difficult for some of us. There are middle-aged men in Charleston right now willing to brag that they never paid to see a single performance at Davis-Brunk. They're lying, of course; Topwater Mulligan was the only one who never had to buy a ticket to see the show.

Under old man Brunk, slipping under the fly hadn't been particularly dangerous. He hired Constable Jack Winters, or in a pinch he even hired Constable Pistol Pete Murchison, to march around outside, but that didn't work. Not really. Jack was almost as much a coward as Pete was, so they stayed out of the way when we mounted a really determined assault upon the fly.

But when old man Brunk's daughter married her leading man, the Davis fellow, it made a difference. Davis immediately began looking for a way to stop leakage as they moved from town to town. I was standing around that Sunday morning, watching the temporary laborers erect the tent under the supervision of the Toby, and that was when I heard the Davis fellow say something to the effect that he wanted to hire the meanest man in town to guard against leakage. Topwater joined me, and we watched and listened as Davis moved from one laborer to the other. They all agreed that there was but one really mean man in town.

"Clodd McCall."

The Davis fellow was an actor, and when he finally stood before me and Topwater, he asked the way actors ask, "What, may I ask, is a Clodd McCall?"

I looked him straight in the eye, and to show him that we could do a little funny talk too, I said, "A Clodd McCall is the meanest son of a bitch in Charleston, Arkansas."

I shouldn't have told him that; my troubles began when I did.

The Davis fellow lighted up like a summer morning, fast. "You tell Clodd McCall I want to see him."

"*You* tell 'im," Topwater said, and his face had never looked quite so sad. "He's looking for the both of us right now."

So Clodd got the leakage job. He was given a badge and a cowboy hat because the Davis fellow thought he would be more authoritative if he looked like a cowboy sheriff. Clodd was also given the authority to arrest anybody trying leakage. "I pronounce you under arrest for leakage," he was supposed to say. Not so many of us attempted to duck under the fly that year.

We didn't dare. I was young enough that I could support black eyes, a broken nose, and caved-in ribs and still remain decently agile, but Clodd was mean enough and fast enough that he would have been willing to chase me halfway to Branch or Bloomer, our neighboring towns, in order to add to my condition. Topwater somehow managed to see the first act of *Tilly's Automatic Washing Machine,* the Monday night offering, but when the lights came up for the candy sale, Clodd caught sight of Top in the reserved seats and asked for his ticket stub. Top reached into his pockets and, his instincts honed, ducked at the same time. Clodd missed and hit a farmer immediately beside Top. The farmer rose, then tottered before he fell, cold-cocked; his wife set up a hell of a howl. If it hadn't been for that woman's caterwauling, Top might have been caught; Clodd never could handle a bawling woman.

His pay was four bits a night. From that, the Davis fellow deducted a dime because he said he had to use it to pay the lighting expenses on Clodd's introduction act. Between the third and fourth acts, immediately after the candy sale, Clodd was introduced from the stage. The Davis fellow even handled the introduction personally: "Ladies and gentlemen, in show business there is always somebody whose labors are essential to the show. You know what I mean? The show must go on!" At this point the drummer, who was also the leading man, began a soft roll on his snare. It increased in volume until Clodd's name was called. "Here in good old Charleston, we have found a man that has done for us a better job than we've run into in a long time. Ladies and gentlemen, our special officer in charge of leakage, *your own Mr. Clodd McCall!*" And with that the trumpet, Toby, blew a short fanfare, and a spotlight fell on Clodd McCall.

He stood at the side of the tent, his back against the fly, and he was miserable. His baggy cheeks and his puckered mouth were both wet, one with sweat and the other from licking. Beneath that hat, which was just a bit too large for him, Clodd didn't look at all dangerous. Indeed, he looked like a man firmly seated on a sizzling stove on which he will stay, come hell or high water, until he no longer needs to prove he can stand the pain. When the light first fell on him, his hands were busy with each other, as if one were trying to chase the other into a natural position, and then when the light struck his eyes, he dropped into an elaborately casual pose which produced a howl of laughter, especially from the Onion Creek rowdies.

"Aw . . ." Top said. Top had a great deal of native sympathy for people who suffered.

But Clodd loved it. He imagined himself a hero, a celebrity. During the daylight hours, wearing cowboy hat and badge, he strode up and down the Street determined to make his image permanent. When a transient stopped to ask for information, Clodd didn't let him finish. "I can see you don't know who *I* am!" And he stalked away.

Top and I were outside, simply lying in the weeds and watching the tent, the night I became inspired. It came to me as a complete plan.

Top didn't like it. "You ain't got that right, boy."

"Between us, we've had a dozen black eyes from Clodd. What're you talking about?"

"That don't give you no right to hurt him." But Top didn't say another word against my plan. He even helped me; he broke into the schoolhouse and borrowed the paddle, which was not in use during summer months.

The paddle was a full inch thick and about four feet long, and it was heavy because it was made of red oak. I planned to use it during the Saturday night special.

It was really special too. The Saturday night audience, "Only you and you alone," was allowed to spend an extra dime so it could watch the special. In it, Toby played the leading role, and his usual role was played by John. It was a short play, two acts, so the candy sale lasted a little longer to give the audience a bargain. Clodd was to be introduced after the candy sale. The audience, as a special treat, was allowed to hang around and help strike the tent and load the trucks.

Clodd's introduction was to be special too. The Davis fellow promised to mention, by name, all of Clodd's kinfolks in the audience, so people from as far out of town as Onion Creek came in claiming kin. In all, there were almost fifty kinfolks in the audience that night. Because this would take a long time and use up a lot of light, the Davis fellow had to tell Clodd that he wouldn't get his four bits on Saturday. That was all right with Clodd.

I shined fourteen pairs of shoes that day, so I had seventy cents in my pockets. Top and I attended as paid admissions. Clodd, his puckered mouth busy, tried to throw us out, but we had ticket stubs. Clodd, stalking rather dramatically about the tent, occasionally waving toward someone as if he were a popular celebrity, kept his eyes on us. During the candy sale, while Top and I were chomping away and thus not entirely alert, I suddenly heard Clodd's voice right in my ear, "First thing Monday morning, boy, I'm buying that shine stand."

Top and I were so startled by the sudden voice that our instincts took over and we were out of the tent before we could get hold of ourselves. We turned to go back in, then we shrugged; we would have been leaving within another minute anyway. We went to the thicket behind the tent where we had hidden the paddle.

Then we heard the drum roll begin. The introduction took some time. Top was kind of hanging back, occasionally murmuring "Awww," but he didn't break and run. I will confess that I too became slightly nervous, but I had effortlessly handled other coups; I couldn't afford to ruin this one. Finally, when the trumpet call came and Clodd took his bow, I was so nervous that I had the strength of ten men.

The situation was perfect. Clodd's bottom was flush against the wall of the tent when I swung the paddle. It landed with a crack louder than any of us ever heard coming from the tardy desk. Clodd's bottom would have felt that blow if the tent wall had been a foot thick.

For an instant there was silence. Then one of the Onion Creek rowdies bellered a laugh, and immediately after that, Clodd himself bellered. It was the wildest yodel

I had ever heard. There was a great deal of anguish in it, certainly, and perhaps a little humiliation and a little more embarrassment, but most of *that* yodel was terrifying anger.

Top and I fled.

I hung onto the paddle, and as we hurried away into the night we heard the ring of laughter and applause in our ears; for a moment there, I think I might have understood an actor's addiction to applause.

Top went directly to his treehouse and pulled the ladder up behind him. I went home. For more than two hours I sat by my mother's bed and listened while she unburdened herself of that crazy hatred she felt toward Charleston. When it was obvious that Clodd wasn't coming after me, I went to bed and, along toward daylight, fell asleep. I went to both Sunday school and church that day, and even if I was a hero to some people, Brother King and Miss Hettie McIntosh both chastised me.

I didn't see Clodd for nearly a week. Finally, prompted mostly by Top, I couldn't stand it any longer; I went to his house. Clodd wasn't hurt; I was relieved to see that. But the snarl was gone from his voice and he didn't automatically ball his fists. His baggy cheeks and his puckered mouth no longer looked like the equipment of a bully; he looked younger, almost girlish.

He nodded, and when he spoke there was a terrible kind of acquiescent quaver in his voice that caused Top to suddenly turn and run. "I knew some of these days I'd bite off more than I could chew, boy, but I didn't think it'd be you."

He didn't explain and I didn't ask him to.

Clodd never left Charleston. There was something wrong with his stomach, so he was never drafted. He stayed at home until his parents died and then he had to find a job. Finally, a few months before the war was over, Miss Hettie gave him a job in her produce store, and there he remains, a strangely placid middle-aged man, married to an equally placid woman who never bore a child for him.

It was at Windy's funeral in 1954 that

Clodd murmured as he stood behind me and we watched Windy's coffin lowered into the ground, "Boy, right now's a good time to tell you I'll never be able to thank you enough for what you done for me."

Hettie
McIntosh

Norris

X

The older people in town said Miss Hettie looked like a Gibson girl. She was tall and healthy and there was a sweetness of repose in her face that was easy to associate with the things we wanted in Charleston. Her features were sensitive and clean with just a touch of rowdiness. She was the only pretty girl we had; she was our debutante. She was regularly invited to social events in Fort Smith, and when we saw her in that glossy Hudson touring car, bags and hat boxes piled in the back seat, we knew she was going to the depot. She always took the train to Fort Smith; Highway 22 wasn't paved until 1933.

Her father was Burl McIntosh. He wanted us to think he was a glum man, a real bulldog, but we knew better; he was too quick to show his pride. He had the Bank of South Franklin and several thousand acres of land on Grand Prairie and more near Lavaca, and there was also the Charleston Produce Company. The only rich man in town. His house was brick; it was on top of a hill west of town, as if perhaps God had put it there so Burl could watch his town. Even during those flush years in the twenties, only a few people owned cars, but Burl owned three: one for himself, one for his wife, and one for Hettie. All of them were Hudsons, thought by Burl to be a better car than either the Packard, which he said couldn't stay in production long, or the Pierce-Arrow.

There was always talk about Hettie, but there was never scandal. Luke Wingate, our mayor, trimmed her hair once every quarter. During her presence in the shop, there was a kind of tender silence; men watched the operation as if they had a personal stake in how good a job Luke did. Hettie didn't wear those flapper dresses, so nobody ever saw her knees as she sat there, our virgin queen, in Luke Wingate's barber chair, but those ankles, clad in white silk, were beautiful; even so, none of us ever stared.

As she walked home from school every afternoon, dressed like no CHS girl had ever dressed before, she was accompanied by as many as five boys at a time, boys from our best families who knew and admitted that she was too good for them. She stopped at the Creasant Drug Store, and Hootie Sturdy himself served her and her entourage cherry Cokes and put them on Burl McIntosh's bill. The more hopeful boys accompanied her part of the way home. There was something about her easy smile and her calm stride and that wonderful hair that lay like two golden ropes down her back, something about that healthy complexion, that made the boys and the rest of Charleston believe that the good times of the twenties would go on forever.

But nobody walked all the way home with her. At the railroad there was a pause — not awkward, because somehow there was never that sort of thing in her presence, or perhaps it has become tenderized by time in this dream — and with an almost timid glance up the hill at that imposing house, those young men realized that hope was the most hopeless thing of all, and thus they murmured excuses, chores, obligations, homework.

She never dated in the sense that other girls her age did. Those girls were desperately looking for the husbands they needed to assure them of that only stability in Charleston, children, but Hettie had no such worries. When the time came, we imagined, Burl would nod to Hettie and she would in turn nod to some handsome young man from Fort Smith and, soon enough, the Methodist Church would turn into a house of flowers some summer afternoon. But if she didn't date, she did have a social life aside from that mystery in Fort Smith: she was put in charge of things. There were pie suppers, wiener roasts, marshmallow roasts, hikes, ghost hunts, cheering squads for the football games; and because of a need for a unifying personality, Hettie was appointed. She was always allowed to appoint her own committees, and she invariably chose three girls and four boys. Somehow those committees never paired off.

She was the valedictorian when she graduated from CHS. Her speech, delivered in that clear alto without suggesting anything but absolute command of every heart in the auditorium, spoke freely of the things important to us that particular afternoon. People had heard of the Crash, even in Charleston, and Burl McIntosh and Clyde Hiatt, the presidents of our two banks, had been heard to caution those inclined to become reckless. But here was Hettie saying, "There is no reason to believe that our prosperity won't go on forever if we will be patient while our beloved country pauses to catch its breath." We believed

Burl McIntosh had written that speech.

But none of us understood why Burl couldn't attend the exercises. He was president of the school board, and during the past fourteen years, it had been his habit to award the diplomas. With his own daughter, the light of his life, valedictorian, it seemed more than merely unusual that he was absent. When Mr. Pennypacker finished with his own say, he recognized Hettie again.

"Permit me to apologize for my father's absence." Hettie's voice was as clear and as golden as the girl herself. "He had to go to Chicago on bank business." That made us feel better; he was helping the country catch its breath.

We never saw Burl McIntosh again. Occasionally stories drifted back to us; he was seen in almost every state in the Union. Those stories continued to reach us long after time's unreasonable terror would have cuckolded him.

The bank examiners were arrested because somehow they had allowed Burl to loan more than ten times the capital of his bank. New examiners were dispatched from Little Rock. Ponderous men with celluloid collars, pince-nez, and banker's breath, they squeaked about in their patent leather shoes to interview almost every adult in Charleston. Finally, they had the terrible truth. The Bank of South Franklin was not only bankrupt; there was hardly any cash on hand at all: a few dollars in silver and several thousand pennies; that was all. Only one piece of paper, a two-dollar bill, was found in a dark corner of the safe.

When Hettie's mother was told the truth, she died. Heart attack, Doc Bollinger called it, but he didn't argue when we called it a broken heart.

Hettie was seventeen. For weeks we didn't see her at all. The blaze of autumn, the only real break in our lives for the next few years, was ignored that year. We watched and waited for her. Nobody was hungry, but our best people were giving away food; old hogs were butchered along with retired milch cows, and sometimes our proudest losers found baskets of food on their back porches.

During the Christmas exercises, Hettie

reappeared. She was Miss Liberty in the pageant, a girl somewhat taller than we remembered, solemn, composed, and she was so pretty she brought tears to our eyes. The day after Christmas, Judge Wilkins appointed people to see after the liquidation of Burl's assets. There was a gesture; Hettie was appointed a referee. The four men, Spread Benefield, Scrooge Wilkins, Luke Wingate, and Windy Spears, later remarked that Hettie quickly took hold, and within days she knew as much about her father's business affairs as any of them did.

We were beginning to worry about finding a charity on which Hettie could feed until she found a husband when she was rescued by a stroke of luck. From somewhere in that distant mystery called the East appeared a man who offered to buy up the McIntosh land. It was simple, he said; he had lost most of his money in the Crash and now he was investing the remainder of his fortune in the one thing, land, that couldn't fall. The check he wrote restored the bank's assets, and there was even a little surplus for Hettie.

The bank examiners transferred those assets to the American State Bank. Bids for the produce company were coming in, too, but Hettie stopped that.

"I'm going to run the produce company." Even when she was being firm, there was a golden quality in her voice.

Windy didn't know how else to put it: "Ain't you fixing to go to the University?"

"Gentlemen, I've discovered I have a talent for business. I have asked Judge Wilkins to appoint you to watch over me till I'm twenty-one."

Unflinching, modest, wearing the smile one expects popular royalty to wear in the presence of the crown's subjects, Hettie walked down that hill every morning at sunrise, opened that corrugated steel building, unlocked the safe, and the business of the day began. In that rambling old building, bemused by generations of odors associated with chickens, beef hides, seed, and feed, she wore flawlessly white dresses with lace and smelled of lavender; before she was twenty-five we had begun to think of her as a kind of lovable institution.

Those young men who had hoped for her attentions fell away into marriages they never would appreciate, but Hettie was still unmarried when she reached thirty. She was still pretty; indeed, if she had chosen to follow the current styles instead of wearing dresses that looked astonishingly like the one she had worn at her graduation, she might have looked eighteen again. That golden hair, parted in the middle and plaited into two golden ropes that reached her waist, remained as bright as it had ever been.

Hettie prospered. Windy Spears, probably the only one in town she encouraged as a friend, once asked her why she didn't hire a manager and trap her a man. She gave him that remarkable smile and then, as serene as ever, tapped his chin with a forefinger. "Oh, come now, Mr. Spears." Thus we had no official reason why she continued to work, but most of us knew anyhow: she had to continue as a symbol.

We needed symbols. There had never

been much money in Charleston, but we had never worried about poverty before. Men stored their pride, and some of them had to keep it in storage for several years. They picked cotton, hoed corn, picked beans, worked in the hay, even followed the harvests up north. We needed Hettie.

She was in charge of the Christmas exercises, and she talked Fay Cooley, local manager of the power and light company, into stringing colored bulbs across the Street in front of the courthouse. She bought hundreds of goodie bags, mesh things filled with two oranges and a full pound of crooked candy; she cautioned Santa Claus, Spread Benefield in a disguise everybody had always seen through, to give them to everybody, even adults, because most of them needed the nourishment from the oranges.

Hettie visited my mother every Sunday afternoon, and during those visits Momma tried to cast aside the hatred that was a part of her insanity. Momma even tried to straighten up her clothing.

Hettie also visited Doc Bollinger's hospital. She cheered all of them up. Even motorists injured in accidents on Highway 22 received her attentions; they peered after her when she was gone as if they wondered why a dirty little old town like ours would have an angel in residence.

In 1938, when she was twenty-five, we thought she would get married. The WPA engineer stood in awe of nothing in or around Charleston. There was a kind of mystery about him too, for when he and Windy Spears caught the robbers of the bank — the American State Bank — the engineer was contemptuously insulting to those who tried to congratulate or thank him. He was a big man with a loud voice and wrong-colored eyes, but most of the women seemed to think there was something threateningly handsome in his face. He stayed at the hotel, and until Old Cat married Charley Boxx, we thought he was romancing her. He was — until Hettie called on Old Cat one October afternoon.

We never knew the details, of course; we knew only the externals. Hettie was such a private woman and the engineer so brutally contemptuous of us that we could never hope to know more. We saw them

151

together in that big Lincoln he drove. When he was with Hettie, the engineer dressed in what we imagined male fashions were likely to be in those mysteries outside Franklin County. He smoked cigars, and occasionally as he drove by he tossed one of them at us and said in that curiously loud voice of his, "Here, boy, keep this hot till I come back for it."

Hettie sat beside him, smiling either politely or serenely — we never could tell which. Once, when he took her to the Creasant Drug Store for a cherry Coke, they sat at one of those marble-topped tables near the prescription counter, and all at once we heard Hettie laugh. We had never heard that before. It was a sound, silver and deep, that for some reason we immediately recognized as hers.

We worried about her. Windy Spears even murmured, for my ears only, that she couldn't be, just couldn't be a fallen woman. Nobody ever said she was, but there were some "Christian women" who probably thought she was.

We worried about her, but in a way we

wanted her to marry that engineer. Perhaps, some of us reasoned, she could remove some of that brutal arrogance of his and maybe even teach him some of her graces. There was also something else, and everybody but the most religious of our ''Christian women'' glumly acknowledged that a healthy woman needs a man in the bed. We couldn't imagine her in such a state, of course; indeed, we couldn't even imagine her in a nightgown.

Then one day the engineer was gone. Barney Stittchen, who was in charge down at the depot, delivered a telegram to him one morning, and before noon, without speaking to anybody but Charley Boxx and Old Cat, with whom he settled his bill, that engineer was gone. Barney had to honor the integrity of a privileged communication and none of us ever knew the actual wording of that telegram, but by artful guesses on our part and meaningful silences on Barney's, we concluded that the engineer's wife, a woman of some substance, had ordered him to Kansas City.

We didn't see Hettie for several weeks. Some of our women called but she wouldn't see them. Only Windy Spears was allowed in the house and he didn't stay long, no longer than it took him to warn her about putting some food in her stomach. He never told anybody a word if anything was there to be told. Her chicken buyer, Jack Spears, Windy's cousin, knew nothing else to do, so he borrowed some change from the bank and took over the produce business.

She returned on Christmas Eve. As serene and as unapproachable as ever, she resumed the operation of the produce business and those civic duties she had assigned to herself. There was some talk about her this time; another war was approaching, the Depression was wilting, and our fears were shifting, so we talked.

But we were kind. By now we had begun to call her Miss Hettie, and if we did talk about her, it was to say that we would have given our bottom dollar if that engineer had never set foot in Charleston.

Not long after her reappearance, that golden hair began to turn. Grayness that would have been mousiness in another woman looked good on Miss Hettie. She continued to call at the Star Barber Shop, and Luke Wingate, using her belt as a measure, trimmed her hair so that it fell to her waist. By the time World War II began, Miss Hettie's hair was snowy white. She remained beautiful, a figure akin to those in the skylight of the Baptist Church, good and kind but unapproachable.

Of course she and Miss Doll were appointed to the War Bond Committee, and she publicly pledged half of her income to the purchase of bonds. She explained, her voice still that cool alto it had always been, that bonds were a better investment than the produce business and not nearly so smelly. That was her only attempt at humor and we roared with laughter.

She wrote to all of us in the service. Her letters were amazing; it seemed as if she had somehow assumed the role of a young mother. She wrote just about the same things we read in the *Charleston Express,* but her style was lively and, occasionally, even funny.

Miss Hettie was, with Miss Doll, our patriotic symbol during the war. Nobody ever heard her say anything nasty about either the Japanese or the Germans, but she somehow managed to sound patriotic when she made speeches. During the war, when our National Guard regiment was removed from its watch in the Aleutians and was shipped for restaging before it was sent to the Pacific, the trains carrying that regiment were rerouted through those hundreds of tiny Arkansas towns where our boys had been born and had lived. The train carrying G Company, pretending perhaps an urgency that had never been real, didn't have time to stop in Charleston. Instead, its whistle wailing urgently but somehow mournfully, it passed slowly through town. Windy Spears had the Legion Post out and standing at attention on the station platform, but to let the boys know that Charleston was still there and still functioning, Miss Hettie was given the place of honor, while the others stood back.

She didn't wave. She just stood there,

erect, an archaic figure in a setting perhaps as archaic then as it is now, and when the train began to pick up speed, she didn't move. She didn't slump; she never had. Nor was there any gesture to tell us that something was wrong, but as that train moved away toward its next little town, its whistle wailing mournfully, people hurried to see what was wrong with Miss Hettie.

She was crying. Her face wasn't distorted; only her mouth was slightly twisted. But her eyes produced enough tears for all of Charleston. Parents took one final look at the train and then, shuffling, murmuring, awkward but determined to comfort her, patted her tenderly. Windy Spears drove her home, and her servant, one of Bessie Grimes Wilkins's daughters, put her to bed. After a while Doc Bollinger arrived and gave her a shot so she could sleep.

Miss Hettie came back to work the next day. She continued with all those frenzied things people do in the name of wartime patriotism, but there was a difference now. Even if she was as serene as ever, there was something tragic in that pretty face. We knew, of course, that it hadn't been the boys on the train. Somehow, during that moment when all of Charleston's young people were gone, she was given a glimpse into her past, and the sight was too much for her to bear.

At the Musterground on the Fourth of July in 1946, she wasn't in charge. She simply read the honor roll. And when Thumb Holyfield's Memorial Day was staged and President Truman was in Charleston, she read Thumb's obituary. When Topwater Mulligan's remains were brought home for reburial, she saw to it that his service was held in the Baptist Church because Top loved the skylight in that church.

There were other services she performed for us. My mother died when I was on Luzon. Miss Hettie and Brother King buried her.

For the same reason that most of the people in Charleston had always been kind to my mother, we never admitted that Miss Hettie might be going crazy. We merely said she was working too hard;

she would be all right as soon as the postwar boom leveled off. But when Windy was buried in 1954 and the funeral seemed to make a shambles of her mind, we stopped pretending.

Even with all but the shadows of her youth and the good order of her mind gone, Miss Hettie remained a beautiful woman. That glistening white hair, now plaited by the Grimes girl; that flawless complexion; those clear eyes. They were all still there. Only her step betrayed the shambles of her mind: the healthy stride was gone and now she reeled about town as if perhaps she had been drinking. Doc Bollinger explained that it was all caused by a stroke or a series of small strokes.

She never became a clown. Even after her flawless memory for names was gone and all faces belonged to strangers, even when she was reduced to calling everybody "customer," nobody ever laughed at her. Jack Spears sometimes teased her about forgetting things, but he did that because she seemed to like it that way.

After she was so old that she couldn't

remember where the produce company was, there was an incident that spelled out somehow, the whole story of Hettie McIntosh. She stopped a stranger, a route salesman, on the Street and asked him for directions to the produce company. "I beg your pardon, customer, could you tell me where I work?"

Thinking she was drunk, the route salesman hooted loudly, but before he could draw breath to indulge himself in another hoot, four Onion Creek rowdies tossed him back into his route truck and told him he would live longer if he never let the eyes of Charleston light upon him again. Another couple of rowdies, all of them middle-aged men now, tenderly escorted Miss Hettie to her office.

Mr. Slim

Norris

XI

He had a Christian name, Elmer, but
nobody called him that. Even his wife, a
plump little woman with a somehow
wizened voice, called him Mr. Slim. He
was a farmer, and during the Depression,
when cotton on at least two occasions
brought as little as a nickel a pound at the
gin, he quit row crops and went into truck
gardening, and because he spent so many
years under that sizzling Arkansas sun, he
was a thin, dark little man by the time he

was fifty; when he died, in his middle nineties, he had always looked impossibly ancient.

Only Mr. Slim's voice didn't age. He was a bass, a booming one, and sometimes on a Sunday morning, just for a straight-faced joke, he would crash down on a particularly deep note in one of the hymns, and that loose pane of glass in the skylight of the Baptist Church would vibrate. Grown-ups were accustomed to it, and because they liked Mr. Slim, they didn't condemn him for having a little fun in church. We children first glanced overhead, alarmed, and then we giggled, because that loose pane of glass just happened to be a part of the Virgin Mary's bottom, and when Mr. Slim boomed his bass note, her bottom wiggled in the bristling summer sun that bathed the interior of that church in holy light.

We children loved him. When for some reason Will Bumpers stopped teaching a Sunday school class at the Methodist Church, more than half of us took up the Baptist view simply because we liked Mr. Slim.

Even after he lost his left eye and began to look more than merely rascally, he remained the sort of wrinkled old man toward whom young people instinctively extend their trust. He planted a dozen rows of watermelons and cantaloupes near the road so we could steal them, and, just to give us a thrill, he invariably caught us and fired his shotgun into the air a couple of times. He raised peanuts too, not because they were a profitable crop but because he liked to roast them so he could leave a huge black-iron pot of them on his front porch, so when we passed, we could help ourselves, even stuff our pockets.

His wife died in 1936. Perhaps Doc Bollinger was as surprised as we were; she appeared at his hospital one winter afternoon and announced that she was going to die, and sure enough she did. The funeral was an event we quickly forgot, but Mr. Slim wore a mourning band on his left sleeve for the remainder of his life. He remained a calm little man, the sort who loved a joke but who wouldn't laugh under any circumstances, and he ran his two hundred acres of land as if he still had that little woman to call him in from the fields when she thought he needed a good drink of well water.

He was never a friend of Spread Benefield's, but they were never enemies either. They both sang in the Baptist choir, and even if they did both sing shaped notes, somehow they just had no time for each other. It was no great matter. Spread repaired our soles and Mr. Slim filled our stomachs, thus they were important parts of our lives. But once a year they came in contact. Spread was Charleston's impresario; during August, he organized and conducted our annual Singing School and Convention.

Mr. Slim didn't participate in the Singing School, although he was easily the best bass in South Franklin County: "I got work to do. I sing on a Sunday, the day the Lord intended us to sing."

But he was willing to furnish the tomatoes. A Singing Convention is an affair not readily understood too far from its native habitat. It begins on a Sunday. There is regular Sunday school, then the preaching, and then a business meeting. For twenty-three years Spread was elected president by acclamation. When the other officers were elected, Mr. Slim was appointed chairman of the Picnic Committee. It was understood that the five women on the committee would round up the fried chicken and the sugar-cured hams and certainly attend to the buying of the puppy-peckers, but the tomatoes were left to Mr. Slim.

The picnic — dinner on the ground — fell on the concluding Sunday. Even those who couldn't stand shaped notes at all did like the picnic. Pork'n beans were furnished in crushing abundance because — well, because they were good and still are. The real delicacy, however, was puppy-peckers, vienna sausages that came eight to the can, eight cents a can, two for fifteen. After gorging ourselves on pounds of chicken and countless thin slices of sugar-cured ham, we finished loading ourselves with pork'n beans and puppy-peckers.

The remainder of the picnic was Mr. Slim's tomatoes. Peeled by the gnarled hands of patient farmwives and then sliced, those tomatoes were huge red wheels that satisfied a craving modern vitamins have never reduced. Heavy copper salt shakers were placed strategically so that the tomatoes could be seasoned.

Mr. Slim allowed nobody else to bring tomatoes. "Y'all just leave the tomaters to me. I don't aim to allow any my friends to eat any them flat, mealy little old things *some* people calls tomaters."

His were the best, unapproachable in excellence. He mixed his own fertilizer and wouldn't even tell his young friends what was in it, but it worked; his tomatoes were sharply acid and firm of texture, and they grew to enormous sizes. Indeed, after experiment showed him just how large he could make them grow, he was obliged to knit little twine bags to hold them on the stakes. Scrooge Wilkins, who served Mr. Slim's vegetables at the Trucker's Cafe, said he had eaten tomatoes all over the country and nothing ever touched what Mr. Slim could do.

He liked to watch people eat his

tomatoes. His good eye, a light blue, actually seemed to have a light of its own when singers already too full of chicken and ham and puppy-peckers staggered back to the tables for just one more helping of tomatoes.

Spread Benefield once said and word got back to Mr. Slim that he aimed to stop the Singing Convention when tomatoes like these were no longer available. From that day until Spread died, the tomato season remained a pleasure to Spread; as Mr. Slim delivered his vegetables to Fort Smith, where he sold that stuff not needed by Scrooge Wilkins, he left a couple of the best tomatoes from yesterday afternoon's picking on Spread's front porch.

Yet the two men never spoke. Mr. Slim brought his boots in occasionally and Spread did repair them. In his stocking feet, Mr. Slim patiently waited until it was time to pay, then he dumped the contents of his bullcod purse on the counter and Spread helped himself. The two men nodded, not unpleasantly, and that was all.

Only once did one of them show any

interest in the doings of the other. A new Baptist preacher arrived. His wife was one of those people who, in a later reincarnation, might be the helpmeet of the manager of a large Chamber of Commerce. Where a Baptist preacher found such a woman and why he would want to marry her was something we couldn't concern ourselves with. She made an effort, during the summer of 1938, to abolish the Singing Convention because she said it made us all look like hicks. We allowed that we were hicks and we didn't mind looking the part. When she couldn't get her way, she attempted to organize it on more cosmopolitan lines. Somehow or other, she found out about Mr. Slim and his tomatoes.

She talked to Spread about it. "Now, Mr. Benefield, don't you think nice little salad tomatoes would look better at the picnic?"

"Ma'am?" Spread wasn't stupid, but when he was startled, not only did his marsupial pouch attempt to crawl upwards, he had a hard time finding words.

"Now don't you think so?"

"Why, no'm, I don't. Singing Conventions come off better if we got good *big* tomaters."

"The preacher's wife made her closing move. "Very well, if we must have big tomatoes, I insist that each one weigh at least two pounds."

By this time Spread's pouch was almost to his chin, and his soft, unwavering eyes were beginning to water. "Piss on you, sister; I ain't asking Mr. Slim to cut his tomaters in two for *no*body."

When Spread died in 1956, Mr. Slim attended the services. He sang with the choir, but his voice was beginning to tire now, and only once could he produce that note that made the Virgin's bottom wiggle. Nobody looked up, but abruptly the singing decreased in volume as if, perhaps, throats were too constricted.

Mr. Slim was the last of the old people to die. Some of us moved away from Charleston, but when we traveled and it was at all possible we stopped at his truck garden; thus he taught an entire new generation. That company in Fort Smith that handled his vegetables began sending a truck to pick them up in 1960 because the sight in his remaining eye was too dim for driving. He put his shabby old truck in the barn and left it there. When he died, some sentimentalist made a wreath of tomatoes which was placed among the hundreds of wreaths that deluged his casket. They were, however, nice little salad tomatoes.

There were no survivors, but Spread's twin daughters and their husbands handled the details of the funeral. They sang, of course; there is always music among Baptists. One of the twins, a grandmother thrice over, reminded us of something we had always taken for granted: "Mr. Slim was Poppa's best friend. Poppa never got over what Mr. Slim could make the Lord's earth do with a little old tomater."

Thumb
Holyfield

Norris

XII

A photograph extant remembers Thumb
when he was in the tenth grade. The
photographer was another one of those
hordes who swarmed into and then out of
tiny little towns in Arkansas during the
Depression, each putting to the test an
economic theory called free enterprise
which was staggering like an Onion
Creek rowdy on a Saturday night. The
photographs were made, and a week later
the photographer reappeared with prints.

171

If sales were good enough to exhaust the supply of prints, the photographer disappeared into that mystery called a darkroom, really a box bolted to the frame of a Model A, and sure enough, more prints were ready within hours.

Thumb was squarely in the middle of the picture. I was on his left, Topwater was on his right and, according to what some people said about us, if Thumb was between us, then he was in the middle of something. Thumb wasn't a mischief maker, nor was he a participant. Things didn't happen to him; they happened around him. He, thumb in mouth, slowly turned and watched.

Because his eyes were large and round and because his eyebrows made almost perfect half-circles, most of us remember him as having worn glasses, but there are no glasses in that photograph, and indeed he was accepted for pilot training before the war began, so he isn't remembered correctly.

He was the only son of a family of eight. His sisters and his mother were all brisk women; not shrews, perhaps not even bullies, but they did abound in energy. They were Thumb's bodyguards, and they were uncommonly efficient. Even Clodd McCall steered clear of the Holyfield sisters and went out of his way to be polite to Thumb.

Thumb's father was a stolid man, morose concerning the national economy. He farmed five hundred acres of cotton and black-eyed peas just south of Nixon Cemetery. He owned three spans of mules, all bays, and by the time Thumb was twelve he could handle a bull-tongue plow, so the Holyfields weren't obliged to pay a hired hand; the oldest daughter could also handle a plow. Not that Thumb was a big boy. Indeed, at first glance, he appeared to be quite frail; it was those soft, wondering eyes. His shoulders were good and his legs were strong. He stood exactly six feet, barefoot.

It was Windy who put it into words about Thumb and his father. "Exactly alike! Both of 'em! When the world comes to an end, old man Holyfield'll be bad-mouthing the Depression and the boy's gonna be pumping on that thumb."

Thumb's right thumb was almost twice the size of his left one. It was soft, white, always clean. He liked to place that thumb's cushion against the roof of his mouth and lightly hook his forefinger over his nose; and with those great soft eyes warmed with the wonder of life, he watched the passage of his peers and his betters. It must have been quite a sight to him: Charleston during the Depression was a swarm of clearly defined characters not easily remembered in dreams. During the summers of 1937 and 1938 Thumb went to summer school in Fort Smith, and that must have given him another warmth to wonder about.

He disappeared during September of 1939. He graduated from high school and then he was gone. We didn't miss him. It was as if he had belonged to a club all his life and had a record of perfect attendance, but his first absence was unnoticed and nobody ever bothered to ask about him. His family continued to appear at church, but nobody ever asked them the whereabouts of Thumb.

It wasn't until I went to the University

of Arkansas as a freshman in 1940 that I saw him again. He was slightly taller, but there was no change in his manner. He stood there, pleased to see somebody from home but not necessarily equipped to chat or gossip. I saw him three times a week; he entered Old Main for a ten o'clock class just as I was leaving for the library.

Then one day the *Charleston Express* received a notice from the Army Air Corps. Hollis T. Holyfield had been accepted for flying cadets; he would train in San Antonio, Texas, and if he completed his training, he would be commissioned a second lieutenant and would wear silver pilot's wings.

''Just like the Army.'' That was Windy's comment; his stories were becoming slightly modernized; criticism of the military was considered wildly funny now. ''That little old Holyfield boy signed up for a hitch and they got 'im mixed up with somebody else.''

And that was all we heard about Thumb for a while. It was as if he were a paper boat some child had thrown into Berry

Creek; nobody expected to see him again and, indeed, hardly any of us remembered him at all.

Then one hot August afternoon in 1942 Thumb flew a B-24 down the Street. It was quiet that afternoon. The war was on and people were at work. The bomber, its four engines roaring and thundering, its long graceful wings seemingly blacking out the sun, gave Charleston a shaking it had never imagined possible, I'm told. It was headed east. It lifted a wing to keep from knocking over the steeple of the Methodist Church, then it made a long ponderous turn and came back down the Street again.

The airplane was so low that the hundreds who came running could see members of the crew grinning and waving. The pilot seemed to be having the most fun of all. I'm told that Windy Spears was pensive for a couple of days and then, seated in the barber shop, suddenly blurted, "You know, the driver of that airplane sure did look like that kid Thumb Holyfield."

Charleston wanted to believe that. The

war was being lost and heroes were needed. Charleston especially needed one. A half-dozen boys from Charleston, hardly more than children who had enlisted to relieve family burdens during the Depression, had been killed at Pearl Harbor or caught in the Philippines. But even if Charleston did want to believe that Thumb was the pilot of that bomber, it was impossible. Nevertheless, the editor of the *Express,* one of the fleshier Colvert sisters, wrote in her weekly column, "Main Street from Here," that it sure did look like Thumb, "another one of the heroes our beloved country can produce when slant-eyed devils and kraut-eating jugheads think they can give us a thrashing." But she didn't run the stories when the Air Corps sent press releases announcing the medals Thumb was winning. She just didn't know who Hollis T. Holyfield was.

Nobody else did either. A lot of our boys died because they were strong and willing and uneducated, perfect infantrymen, and there were parents who dreamed of their sons getting into the Air Corps because death there seemed somehow better than it did in a foxhole. By the time the war was another year old, Charleston had forgotten Thumb Holyfield completely.

Then one afternoon in the spring of 1945 an Army sedan came to town. That wasn't unusual, because Camp Chaffee was just a few miles away. But from this sedan stepped a major general. Windy, busy updating his lies in the faces of those few soldiers home on furlough, almost fainted when the general entered the Creasant Drug Store. Windy recovered, popped to attention, and gave his best salute; he had never laid eyes on a general in his life.

"Private Jasper S. Spears, 19099225, reporting, sir." Windy's voice, they told me, had never sounded quite so gassed before. "Anything I can do for the general, sir?"

There was a lot Windy could do for the general. He was here to arrange perhaps the greatest event in Charleston's history. The president, President Harry Truman, would appear in some twenty days to attend the funeral of Major Hollis T. Holyfield. Windy was allowed to know

178

that, before the coffin was lowered into the grave at Nixon Cemetery, the president would place on it the Congressional Medal of Honor. The medal wouldn't be buried with the coffin, of course, but nobody misunderstood the gesture.

And that's what happened. The Holyfield family, that stolid father, all those brisk women, were shrouded in black and the president kissed the women and embraced the father. He told them all that he would rather have had that medal than be the president of the United States. Windy Spears, as a local gesture, was put in command of that honor guard of crack infantrymen who fired the salute over the grave. A military bugler blew Taps, and from the white oaks over the hill a cornet player from the Charleston Tigers Band played Echo.

The president, the reporters, the photographers, the security troops and that major general were gone before sundown. Only an Air Corps detachment remained. It was under the command of an almost adolescent captain. It turned out that he had been in the raid over Truk when Thumb was killed.

"Old Hollis caught a burst of flak right between engines one and two, but he bored right on in. He did salvo his bombs instead of pecking them out in order, but he managed to get over the target and he did the most damage. The rest of us throttled back and poked along so we could stay with him; the fighters kept on us almost two hundred miles. Hollis and his boys got three fighters.

"He made it back to base on two engines and he made a perfect landing too. Greased it in! Nobody even knew he was wounded till he taxied into his revetment, then he died before they could get him out of the plane."

"I'll declare," Windy breathed.

"I'll bet nobody in Charleston was surprised when old Hollis pulled something that wild and woolly."

Windy was as capable of speaking for Charleston as anybody else. "Yes sir, we all knew that boy was wild and woolly. Them slant-eyed devils're probably glad he ain't still alive.

"The young captain wagged his head, fraught with admiration and nostalgia. "There's a lot of broken hearts now that old Hollis is dead. I never saw a guy with so many women in love with 'im."

Windy laughed heartily. "Yes sir, captain, that boy was a stud! A regular *stud!*"

And that's the lie we're still telling. Some of our women, at middle-age now and some even grandmothers, blushingly confessed that their virginity had more than once been threatened by Thumb Holyfield. A few others, by accident of nature never virgins at all, are quick to admit that their first was Thumb. Most of us managed to compose stories that, according to our invididual lights, found Thumb to be a boy adventurer, a salty talker, a real American boy.

Windy Spears passed the hat, and soon enough money was found to erect a votive monument, an obelisk, on the courthouse lawn. It isn't far from the Robert E. Lee statue, right next to the deer. There are monuments elsewhere on the lawn, the Honor Roll from the Confederacy, from both world wars, from Korea and now Vietnam, but Thumb's is special; he was our only pilot. Top also won a Medal of Honor, but the president didn't come to Charleston when Top was buried. Thumb's is special because it is so imposing.

It is thirty feet high and it looks like a sword pointed into the sky. Its base is some fifteen feet square, and on each of its four sides is embossed the name Hollis T. Holyfield. A pair of silver pilot's wings are imbedded in the stone immediately under each rendition of the name. The dates of his life and the citation awarding him the Medal of Honor are on the front side of the monument. Immediately above the citation, the tombstone artist embossed a likeness of Thumb taken from that picture made of his class when he was in the tenth grade. The likeness wears glasses.

Topwater
Mulligan

Major
Billings

Norris

XIII

Topwater Mulligan was the best friend I ever had in my life. He was one of those things, those events people accepted because, instinctively, we knew that in one way or another everything he did was right.

He lived in a tree. It was a willow oak, sometimes called a pin oak, *Quercus phellos,* a monumental tree that grew in the front yard of old Major Billings's house. That old tree, mounting to the heavens in a kind of sprawling dignity, was somehow or other appropriate as a home for Top, and it was also appropriate that it would be found in the Major's front yard. All three were unique to Charleston.

Top had the face of a basset hound, and even though he was my age, he looked like an old man when the rest of us were still bragging about having some pubic hair. Somehow, Top's skin was too big for him, as if perhaps a skin salesman had in stock a covering that would have fitted a taller, wider man. Top's eyes were kind of a gentle blue. His nose was large, bulbous, fully rounded. His eyebrows slanted over the nose as if they formed a slanted roof. I have never seen anybody quite so sad, at a glance, and I have never known anybody quite so kind.

Nor have I ever known anybody who had more fun. Top was friendly with every dog in town. Indeed, some of our more vicious dogs were Top's guards when he sneaked into henhouses to steal eggs, so Top was never entirely without money. Miss Hettie and Jack Spears knew the eggs were stolen — Top delivered them for sale in his overall pockets — but Miss Hettie liked him, just as everybody else did, and she knew Top had to eat.

There is no doubt that Top was the only habitual thief in town, but to redeem him, there was a certain Robin Hood motif in his style. If he stole a dozen eggs from somebody, he left half of the proceeds on the victim's front porch, where it could be found at daylight. When he stole watermelons or cantaloupes from Mr. Slim, he invariably warned Mr. Slim that the theft would take place at a certain time of the day. And it did.

He became friendly with Major Billings because Top blew up a bee tree. The tree, a white oak, *Quercus alba,* was filled with honey from root to crown, but it was too tall for us to get safely at the honey. We needed dynamite. I didn't even know how to spell the word. Top knew no more. But he stole a case of it from the Hardware, and after we talked it over and after we did some reading in the school's *Book of Knowledge,* we decided that the tree would require an entire case to be properly blasted.

A particularly large hunk of honey landed on Major Billings's front porch. The Major was waiting when we reached his house.

The Major asked me to stay, but I had never laid eyes on a face that wild, so I hurried on home.

Top stayed. He and the Major spent the entire night on the Major's front porch. The Major's daughter raised hell, but according to Top, the old man didn't seem to hear her at all. Top and the Major didn't go to bed at all that night. From that night on, Top concentrated on the Major almost as much as he did on advertising.

Advertising amused Top. Not in newspapers. I don't suppose Top ever read anything except what Miss Doll assigned. It was signboards that amused Top. Those one-sheets at the Gem Theater were particularly attractive to him; he could overhaul a picture of Clark Gable or Joan Crawford so handsomely that those stars, when the Gem's owner, Carl Dozier, sent to them what Top had done, wrote him a fan letter and asked for more. Top ignored them.

He liked signboards along Highway 22 best. Ewell Shelby, one of the few entirely civilized filling station operators in Arkansas, liked to hire Top to do those little jobs that had a kind of natural entertainment value. One day Ewell was told the awful truth; Top had turned all of Ewell's signs upside down. For days Ewell was in a swivet, but when he began to notice that motorists were ponderously telling him about his crazy signs, he left them as they were; he was selling more gas. Some of the signs, hardly more than peeling boards now, are still along the highway.

During summers, Top liked to force his way into the schoolhouse and draw on the blackboards. There was room after room of walls covered with blackboards. His pockets sagging with different colors of chalk, Top covered those boards with pictures. Most of them were animals playing in the woods, but occasionally, if one looked closely, situated somewhere in the woods would be a small boy, hardly more than a baby, pissing on a flat rock.

When the teachers showed up for fall orientation, the arguments were invariably bitter. Mr. Pennypacker wanted the boards cleaned immediately. Miss Doll wouldn't have it; she wanted the children to see the pictures before the regular business of teaching got under way.

Top attended church every day of the week except Sunday. He liked the gloaming silence of the churches, and he was especially fond of the Baptists, because their stained glass windows were the best. On a bright sunny day he sometimes spent as many as six hours quietly seated in his favorite pew looking at the windows. On certain days of the year, the summer solstice and the three days that preceded and followed it, he liked to lie on the floor of the Baptist sanctuary and gaze at the skylight with its fanciful flights of heavenly hosts

Top had parents, but they had long ago given up on him. He left home when he was hardly thirteen. He didn't run away from home. He just left. If his parents, his three sisters, and his seven brothers wanted him, all they had to do was look around; he rarely left town. But he didn't go home. For several years he slept in the mulebarn, but the Clodd family didn't like that: Top's corncob pipe might set the hay afire. And for a month or so he slept in the warehouse of the Charleston Hardware. It was a warm, dry place, and Will Bumpers didn't mind because Top kept the place clean, and he wouldn't let the Onion Creek rowdies steal the place bare either.

Top was sixteen when he moved into the tree.

The tree was a challenge, but the rest of us stayed out of it because we somehow imagined that old Major Billings wouldn't like it if we messed around on his property. He had been shot through the ankle at the Battle of Murfreesboro shortly after Christmas of 1863 and he carried a cane. He used that cane once: one of the Scarbrough brothers tried to rob the bank and the Major hospitalized him for three months. If the Major was that good with the cane, we reasoned that we had better stay away from him.

But because of the honey incident, Top

was the old man's friend. We were walking down North Greenwood Street one hot afternoon when we heard a cardinal singing in the Major's tree. "If it's cool enough for that bird to sing in that tree, that's where I'm headed." And Top squirreled up that tree with no effort at all. I didn't hang around.

Top was still in the tree when the Major found him. "Hey, Top, what you doing up there in my tree?"

"Just setting."

The Major thought that over. "What's it like?"

"Cooler than it is down there."

The Major was eighty-two at the time, but he didn't give a damn; he went to his barn and fetched a ladder. He and Top spent the remainder of the afternoon seated on a huge limb. They talked and the Major chewed and spat. After a while Top fished his drawing paper out of the bib of his overalls and did some sketches of the Major. When the Major's daughter came home, she raised hell; she was the only Charleston native who ever spoke harshly to Top. The Major cussed her roundly, but finally she begged him to come down and, nimbly enough, he scampered down the ladder.

By daylight Top was in the tree again. This time I was with him. I didn't know what he was up to and I didn't really care; I was so proudly flattered to be his only close friend that I never bothered him with questions. We carried several boards Top had stolen from the O'Bar Lumber Company and we had a bag of nails Will Bumpers thought were a little too rusty to sell. I picked up a hammer at my house. Before the day was over I knew what Top had in mind: we had a floor and a roof on his treehouse.

We finished the walls and installed the windows the next day. It was the first house in Charleston to be equipped with insulation against the cold; Top stuffed burlap into the walls. There was only one room at first because Top wanted to finish a snug place for the Major to sit while we worked. Within four days we had added two more rooms. We could sit up there out of the heat, and the Major could chew and spit and try to match Windy's record as

Charleston's crack liar.

It was late August before we decided to add a porch, and that was as big as the house ever got. At first people were jealous of us; they wanted an invitation. But Top wasn't the sort people dropped in on, and the only invitation he and the Major ever issued was to me. Top did discuss the possibility of asking Will Bumpers and G. H. O'Bar to a housewarming because they had furnished the materials for the house, but nothing ever came of that. Finally, as people in Charleston would, they got used to us, and the jealousy drifted away in those mists of stories told about Topwater Mulligan. People occasionally sniffed as they passed, but they were just sniffing at the odor of the food; Top was the best cook in South Franklin County.

That fall I went to the University. I didn't see Top and the Major again until Thanksgiving. The Major had fallen, and his ankle, the war wound, was so severely injured that he could no longer walk, so Doc Bollinger rounded up some labor and, as the Major demanded, he was hoisted up to Top's house by a system of ropes and winches. The Major was there to stay. Top made countless pencil sketches of the Major's wild old face and stacked them in a corner with all his other work.

When I returned to school after the holidays, I took a lot of Top's work with me. An art professor at Fayetteville, David Durst, didn't hesitate. He drove to Charleston. He spent a pleasant afternoon and evening with Top and the Major. Durst was one of those peculiarly sensitive men who understood easily such people as Top and the Major, so he made no effort to teach Top anything; he was convinced that Top already knew all he wanted to know.

I might have grown away from my origins (shine boys do that) as I broadened my rural education, but I never got those people out of my mind, especially Top and the Major. Top and I fished Berry Creek that Christmas for the catfish he liked to deep-fry and serve with hushpuppies and buttermilk. The next summer we stole watermelons from Mr. Slim, and after they were cooled by the night winds, we ate them for breakfast. During those vacations just before the war began I spent as much time in Charleston as possible, and during our hours together neither Top nor the Major asked one question about college life. Their lives in the tree were full, fraught with good Civil War stories and the delights of stolen food; in the secrecy of their imaginations, they must have thought I was enduring a terribly dull life in Fayetteville.

Top made sure my mother took her medicine, the only attention she needed. He tried to talk to her; he even listened to her reasons for hating everybody in Charleston, but neither of them mentioned my education. Nor did the Major.

Not until I was drafted did Top and the Major show any interest in that life I led outside the city limits of Charleston. The Major was as much an authority on the military life as Windy Spears, and his advice was as good as any I ever heard; it was also, word for word, exactly the same advice Windy gave me: "Keep your bowels open and your mouth shut." The Major had a wild old time expounding on that philosophy, but the lies he told would have become a part of our national folklore if they had been put to paper.

When Top went to steal a pound of coffee, the Major's attitude changed. "Boy?" he said to me. He was serious for the first time since he and Top had moved into the tree.

"Yes sir?" I moved closer to the Major.

"Top'll get drafted too, won't he?"

"Probably, yes sir."

The Major shook his head, and somehow that gesture expressed as profound a sorrow as I had ever known. I was prepared to hear something else, but the Major said, "I wonder how old Top'll ever get along without me to look after 'im."

Top was drafted, sure enough. Doc Bollinger rounded up some labor again and the Major was removed from the tree. He was installed in a huge rocker situated in the bay window of his house where he had a breeze in the summer and could be kept warm in the winter.

Top was a terrible soldier. There was

nothing the Army could do with him. They put him in the stockade, but that was no worse than barracks life to Top. They put him on KP for ninety days, but they had to take him off that because he was stealing them blind. Finally somebody came up with a brilliant idea: Why not punish this man by giving him combat duty? That was the kind of Army we had.

Top was immediately a hero. As soon as his unit landed on the island of New Britain, Top disappeared. Somehow or other, he managed to blast to smithereens Japanese bunkers that would have caused the death of hundreds of Americans. That must have been as much fun as the bee tree had been. He got a Distinguished Service Cross for that.

He was in seven island campaigns. During the last four, he belonged to a secret sneak-and-snoop organization with the somewhat mundane name of Alamo Scouts. For each of the campaigns, he received at least one medal, but keeping Top out of jail when he wasn't in combat was a real problem. Finally General Kreuger solved that problem: he commissioned Top a captain. According to men who served with him, Top thought his commission was the only genuinely funny joke he had ever participated in.

Nobody ever knew the real circumstances of Top's death. During the first days of the Luzon campaign, he was put ashore on a mission with something to do about the Ipo Dam. Two months later his body was found on a jungle trail near that dam. There was a single wound, a small one immediately above the right eye, and the Japanese had left him where he had fallen.

Because legends had sprung up around him, President Truman ordered his remains flown home. Sentiment went even further: I was flown home too on the same plane to command an honor guard made up of Charleston boys who had served in the Pacific. President Truman sent a personal message: even if Charleston had done him proud at the funeral of Thumb Holyfield, another trip to this town was out of the question.

The Major, his wild old mind terrorized by time now, roused himself from his senile stupor long enough to recognize me, but more often than not he thought he was talking to Top. I had my four soldiers pick up the Major's chair and we marched off through the falling leaves of autumn. The Major let his mind drift during the drive to Nixon Cemetery, but occasionally he collected himself and remembered those remarkable breakfasts we had enjoyed in the treehouse.

As we stood there, the graveyard bemused by thousands of falling leaves, I could see, immediately below the preacher's right elbow, my mother's grave, and somehow the pattern I had yearned for disappeared; my life in Charleston hadn't needed a pattern. Top in his coffin, Windy at stiff attention with those men who called themselves Legionaires, and the Major at my side — it was all pattern enough. Miss Hettie and Miss Doll stood across the grave, watching me.

The Major suddenly stirred just as the preacher finished his benediction. ''Boy . . .'' His voice had always been old, but now it was ancient.

I knelt by his rocker. "Yes sir?"

"That wouldn't be old Top in that box, would it?"

"Yes sir."

"How'd he die?"

"In the war, Major."

"Aw pshaw! Top wasn't in the war!"

"There's been another one."

"Oh." The Major worked on that for a while. "Who we fighting?"

"The Japanese and the Germans."

The Major couldn't handle that. "Who're the Japanese?"

"They — well, they live in the Pacific. Very far away."

"Must be pretty hod-damn far. I never heard of 'em." The Major was making a terrible effort to make his mind march straight and at the proper interval, but he couldn't manage it. "Old Top must of stole something they had a value on, else they'd not have a reason for killing 'im."

"No sir."

The Major didn't last much longer. His daughter was dead and his house was caving in. When Will Bumpers was killed by a fool drunk driving a car, there was nobody to see after minor repairs. One of Doc Bollinger's nurses had better work offered elsewhere, but she stayed with the Major until he died.

He left a will. There was some money, all of it stipulated as to dollars and cents: So much for G. H. O'Bar, whose lumber had been stolen for the treehouse; so much to Will Bumpers's heirs for the nails; a little bit here and there to Mr. Slim for the vegetables we had stolen. Top and the Major had kept good books. I was the principal beneficiary and executor; the house was mine, and the young lawyer, one of Will Bumpers's two sons, both of whom had become lawyers, displayed great aplomb when it was understood that the house in question was situated in a tree.

The funeral itself was as grand a thing as Charleston had ever seen. The president wasn't there but almost everybody else was: Senator Fulbright, Senator McClelland, and all of our congressmen. Our governor, a Pacific veteran who had somehow heard of both the Major and Topwater Mulligan, prevailed upon the state general assembly to pass a special law promoting the Major to Brevet Colonel and then another special law allowing him to be buried among the roots of the tree below the house. Arkansas politicians are generous about that sort of thing.

Tangle-Eyes

Norris

XIV

Her real name was almost lost in those mists that arose in the early years of the Depression. She was born in 1911, so by the time the Crash came she was already a grown woman, expected to have been married and a mother by the time the Bank of South Franklin failed, which was how Charleston measured the beginning of that peculiar decade that preceded World War II. We called her Tangle-Eyes.

She was kin to several people in town.

Somehow or other, she was a cousin to such people as Windy Spears, Topwater Mulligan, and Melmer Dunmore. She was Spread Benefield's niece. She also shared a common ancestor with Miss Hettie McIntosh. None of them denied her, because Tangle-Eyes didn't make it a practice to talk about her kinfolks, but sometimes she passed them on the Street and called them by their family nicknames. It is to the everlasting credit of her kinfolks that none of them ever snubbed her.

Her mother was the agent of the family connections. She had been a collateral Benefield, the family founding Charleston, but she had had bad luck with the flu epidemic of 1918, so Tangle-Eyes was a half-orphan when she was seven. Almost everybody in Charleston agreed that the death was more than a tragedy; her father was Ransom Olds. He was neither Methodist nor Baptist. He wasn't even a Presbyterian. He was a Holy Roller, even if he was never holy and didn't even roll except on those occasions when he went to church drunk.

Ransom owned a farm but he wasn't a farmer. He rented it to Mr. Slim and lived on the rental. That meant, of course, that he could sneak onto his land in the dead of night and gather vegetables enough that he could take home, and, sure enough, Tangle-Eyes canned them in those Mason fruit jars Ransom stole in one way or another. So even if he had an income of no more than two hunred dollars a year, Ransom could spend all of it on drink because there was always plenty to eat.

He looked like a pirate because he was small, wore a patch to cover that place where his right eye should have been, and because, damnit, he was a pirate. Our iceman, Amil Curzon, once offered Ransom a ride to Fort Smith to pick up the regular load of ice, and, sure enough, Amil found himself making trips to such places as Lavaca and Greenwood before he finally found his way to the Ward Ice Cream Company in Fort Smith, where he was an hour late. He explained that Ransom didn't actually highjack him; it's just that Ransom had pressing business that had nothing to do with

Amil's destination.

So we weren't surprised when Tangle-Eyes didn't turn out well. She was not, however, Charleston's Belle Watling; she was generous to the point that there was no price, but she was selective enough that there were no strangers either. A kept woman, certainly, and kept by several, but unkept by strangers.

Tangle-Eyes worked hard; she took in washing and ironing, she did practical nursing, and she baked and decorated cakes. Her work was absolute perfection. Those collars she starched were carefully trimmed of frays before she ironed them so that there would be no saw-tooth edge cutting at the neck. Her nursing was accompanied by a supply of broths, beef or chicken or pork — and she had one that we suspected too. But Doc Bollinger was the one who went after her at the onset of a sickness that might proceed unto death, so we knew that Tangle-Eyes knew some of Doc's magic elixers. There isn't a middle-aged woman of any social pretense at all who doesn't look back upon at least one of her teenage parties without remembering those cakes, huge, covered with candles as large as those seen at Christmas services now, basically white but decorated with a multiple whimsey of colors that somehow always became soft and nice and feminine and festive when the candles were lighted.

There wasn't a married woman in town who hadn't damned her, and more than just a few had even called her "that cross-eyed bitch." But there were others who, in their own ways, recognized her as an angel of one kind or another; besides her nursing, Tangle-Eyes had softened the tempers of husbands when women needed a soft-eyed man.

She liked me. She wore high-button shoes, and every other Friday she brought them to me for shining. They were old things with fancifully shaped heels but she took good care of them. She wore them once a week. To church. Perched on that ancient bay mule Ransom used as a façade for his farm, facing backward so she could lean against Ransom's shoulders for support, she rode to church every Sunday morning, those high-button

206

shoes held daintily aside, and not until her feet were assuredly planted on solid ground did she slip into them, work the buttons, and, her left eye looking right and her right eye looking left, enter the church of her choice.

Ransom fished a pint bottle of home-made out of his pocket and, his back against the wall, waited behind the ice house until her worship was complete. She was in charge of the bay mule on the way home because Ransom was slung, face down, behind her: a pint of the stuff he drank was good enough for a full twenty-four hours of oblivion.

We all admitted that Tangle-Eyes might be special because she never got the Holy Ghost. Those Holy Rollers took the Holy Ghost seriously. They were regularly afflicted by it. One of their preachers, who enjoyed an unprecedented tenure of three years in their pulpit, regularly brought off a miracle of such duration that we finally accepted it for what it really was, a miracle. Wearing black-and-white wingtip shoes with taps on heels and toes, he did a dance on that red-hot wood-burning heater the Holy Rollers used to heat their sanctuary. He sometimes stayed up on that thing, an iron monster three feet wide and seven feet long, for as much as thirty minutes, tapping out a little Fred Astaire dance and speaking in tongues.

As he danced, Tangle-Eyes clapped her hands in time to the hymn, a thing called "Glory Take Our Hands and Tongues," but this was a show to her, not a hysterical indulgence. And that's the man she married.

The congregation promptly fired him.

His name was Henry Goforth, and not a one of us ever found out where he came from. He had just appeared in Charleston one morning, hitchhiking and wearing those black-and-whites he was so fond of. He asked around and found out the names of the deacons in charge of holy rolling in Charleston.

They tried him out two nights later. Because Henry hadn't eaten a bite since his appearance in Charleston, he had become somewhat hysterical, so his first sermon was a thing nobody, not even a

Holy Roller, really expected. He quoted, accurately, the thirty-fourth chapters of New Testament books that had only thirty-three chapters. He was as glib in tongues as most of us were in English.

Brother King married them. "I'll marry any couple with a legal license," Brother King told us, one time after another, "and if that foolish little man and that woman want to bind themselves in holy matrimony, I'll not only marry them, I'll ask the Trinity to bestow blessings on them."

Ransom promptly made a criminal of him. Henry was not one of those people instinctively a thief. He was caught by Mr. Slim, of all the people in Charleston. Jack Winters, our constable, caught him trying to devise a way to fetch pennies out of that lone gum machine in front of the Creasant Drug Store that had been there so long that none of us dared put its contents in our mouths. Miss Hettie regularly chided him about the eggs he brought to her produce company; like Topwater, Henry delivered those eggs in his pockets. On a special Saturday night, such as once every summer when Brunk's Comedians came to Charleston, Henry appeared at the produce company with a chicken. Miss Hettie paid him his price, fifty cents, and put the chicken in a special coop so it could await the claims of its rightful owner.

Tangle-Eyes was ashamed of him; she was a Christian woman. But she was amused by him too. When he was caught, she joined Ransom in that wild paroxysm that totally baffled Henry. He wanted them to take him seriously; countless congregations had. But perhaps the only time she ever took him seriously was when he decided to sign up for our National Guard regiment.

In 1939 a private could drill once a month and at the end of each quarter he could draw an unencumbered eleven dollars. That was more money than might be imagined. There were families eating rather well because as many as three or four sons were drawing that money.

Tangle-Eyes was proud of him. "You orta see the look on that funny little old face of his when he comes home with that eleven dollars, boy." She paused to push my cowlick out of my eyes. "Oh, I know. Nobody in Charleston thinks much of him, but he's more than nothing."

I told her the truth. "I kind of like him."

And she kissed me. Tangle-Eyes was that kind of woman, sentimental, affectionate, kind of soft and good. "Why, sure you do! Topwater does too, don't he?"

"I guess so."

"Top must have some kind of feeling for 'im: he's drew a thousand pitchers of Henry's face."

"Yes, he has."

"Are they good pitchers?"

I shrugged. "I guess so," I said. "Yes, they're good pictures."

"Did you show any of 'em to Miss Doll?"

"A couple."

"What'd she have to say?"

"She liked 'em."

"Miss Doll's a good woman, ain't she?"

And I said something I had no authority to say, because I had never heard Miss Doll even so much as mention Tangle-

Eyes. "She likes you too, Tangle-Eyes."

Tangle-Eyes glowed, then she giggled, as if her name were a monumental joke. "She's the only one that wouldn't call me anything but by my right name."

"Is she?"

"Civility."

"Is that your name?"

"Civility Motherwell Olds," Tangle-Eyes said. "That's what my mother named me. She didn't figger I turned out — with eyes each looking the wrong way."

I never called her by another name. Civility was right. It was the way some people are called Jasper but finally become Windy. Or Francis and become Boy. Or Leon and become Dale. She did have eyes that were a terrible tangle, but she was Civility.

And that was when I began looking at Civility as a real person. Her father died that winter. Ransom. There was no money to bury him, but Will Bumpers put him into the ground and Brother King read over him. Topwater and I, not yet out of our middle teens, were pallbearers. We both called her Civility after that. We never took up for her when those jokes were told, but we made it a point not to laugh. And neither did we see anything funny about the fact that an ancient Methodist preacher had buried a one-eyed Holy Roller pirate; after all, his own church refused to bury him, and Top, Brother King, and I reasoned that any man had a right to a formal passage back to the earth.

But Civility never looked at Henry as a real person. "Oh now, y'all know old Henry. He ain't much, but that's all right; he don't want to be much. He preached because that'uz all he could imagine, and when a man's hungry, he got an imagination on 'im like a cat trying to mouse an elephant. Y'all jist don't worry about Henry; he'll be all right long after most y'all're buried out there at Nixon."

Meanwhile, she took in washing and ironing and surplus lust. Men laughed at her crazy eyes but they didn't laugh loud. And as World War II approached, because they were accustomed to her, various wives had begun to accept her in much the same spirit they accepted that cow in the back yard, needful of attention but kind of a necessity.

Civility was one of the few people who could make my mother take her medicine. Momma had problems in her head, and in 1939 there was not a really effective medicine that would do much for those bursting blood vessels. It was a green stuff, sticky with sugar to hide its hideous taste, and it had to be administered at least four times a day or my mother would become a vegetable, and soon enough she would die.

It was Miss Hettie who raised the money for me to attend the University of Arkansas, but it was Civility who gave Momma her medicine four times a day, daylight and dark. Somehow, Civility found daylight time from her washing and ironing, and darkness time from Henry and those other men who called upon her, to make her way to that little house on North Greenwood Street. Twice during the daylight hours, twice at night.

Brother King was explicit. "Angel, first class, boy. She's made a joke out of adultry, but I'll just bet there might be more than one angel in Heaven with a past history of adultry. There're a few people in Charleston you'd be nothing without, boy, and that includes Miss Doll and Miss Hettie, but without Tangle-Eyes, you wouldn't even have a chance to be nothing."

"Yes sir," I said. "Did anyone ever tell you her real name, Brother King?"

"Now, boy, do you figger I'd call a lady Tangle-Eyes if I knew her name?"

"Civility Motherwell Olds Goforth."

"Civility!"

"Yes sir."

"That was Martha's first name." Brother King's wife had been dead less than a year, and his eyes still clouded when he mentioned her name. "Come to think of it, Martha was a little crosseyed when she was a belle." He put his hands on my head. "Now how'd you find out her real name?"

"She told me."

"I see." Brother King nodded a couple of times. "Seems to me a woman'd not tell you a name like that unless that's what she aims for you to call 'er."

"Yes sir."

"Does Topwater call 'er Civility?"

"Yes sir."

"What does your mother call 'er, boy?"

"When her mind's clear enough, Momma calls 'er Mrs. Goforth," I said. "When Momma was a girl, she knew a great lady named Goforth."

Brother King nodded several times, his craggy old face illuminated with a kind of satisfaction that not many people in Charleston will remember him for. "So do you, boy." He took my head in both his huge old hands and shook it gently and then he was gone.

When our regiment was mobilized in 1941, there were officers in Headquarters-and-Headquarters-Company who didn't want Henry Goforth to go to federal duty. Nobody knew why. Perhaps one of us, a somebody not likely to ever identify himself or herself, wanted to reject Henry. We were still patriots then, and there were people who drew the line before others they didn't deem morally worthy of serving our country. Everybody understood that.

Everybody also understood that a man rejected could be represented by somebody willing to testify in behalf of his character. Without too much trouble, Civility rounded up Brother King, Will Bumpers, Spread Benefield, and Scrooge Wilkins. Windy Spears, concerned with the military image in his background, found out about it and insisted on going along. They all presented themselves to Colonel McAllister, who commanded our regiment, and when the regiment actually departed for federal duty Henry was in ranks.

Civility bloomed with pride. She was quick to assure any and all of Charleston that he was worthless but she was proud. "Think of the fun that fool's having!"

I was gone when the regiment went to Alaska. I was in the South Pacific, and by then Charleston had begun to devote itself to that exercise of passion called patriotism. They pretended that Alaska was a dangerous theater, even when they knew nothing was going to happen up there. And when the Japanese gave up on our fortress there and when our regiment was brought back for retraining before shipment elsewhere on the globe, Charleston even pretended that our boys had been retrieved from horror by a miracle.

Nobody will ever know who that genius was who saw to it that our regiment was routed through Arkansas on its way to those various training camps in Texas, but that man did more for civilian moral (and the sale of war bonds) than any functionary in our country's history. There were several trainloads of them, all carefully routed through those dozen-upon-dozen of tiny little towns that had produced the willing boys who had sprung forward so eagerly when the regiment was federalized.

When G Company came through Charleston, our people had been told that our boys "might" happen along that day if anybody just happened to be at the depot around two o'clock in the afternoon. Sure enough, proceeding at great speed, as if to assure Charleston that the railroads were serious about getting our boys to one fighting front or another, our train approached from Doctors Ford Creek with its whistle wailing mournfully.

The train slowed to a speed too fast for some hysterical woman to jump on and slow enough for every parent and wife in town to catch a glimpse of those broadly grinning faces.

On the station platform was Windy in charge of a rigidly saluting detachment of Legionaires in their World's War I leggings and gooseneck collars and Smokey-the-Bear hats. Not far away from him was Miss Doll, because there wasn't a man among them who hadn't studied in her classroom. And then, of course, nearest the train, because she was our queen, was Miss Hettie.

But as our train approached, something prompted Miss Doll to turn, find Civility's face in the crowd, fetch her forward, and stand there holding Civility's hand as our train paraded through our town.

Not many noticed, because Miss Hettie was so emotionally stricken by the passage of our boys, but on the platform of the last car, his feet clad in black-and-white wingtips, pecking out his little tap dance, was Henry Goforth. Without hesitation Civility put a finger to each corner of her mouth, and there was an ear-splitting whistle. Henry promptly stopped his dance. As the train disappeared toward east-southeast, picking up speed, its whistle still wailing with that music that was somehow a part of our decade, most of the Charlestonians there that day will remember the last they saw of the train carrying the last they saw of a son or a husband or a sweetheart — it was tiny little Henry Goforth standing there waving.

Henry died in no battle. He never rose above the rank of private. Nor was he decorated for bravery. The regiment knew what to do with him. He spent most of the war on KP until Colonel Mack happened across him, then Henry became a cook's helper.

Civility received him as a hero. "He wudn't nothing when he left and he ain't much else now, but he given all he had when the country needed it."

They flourish still. Henry so regularly appeared at the Veterans Administration

Hospital on Roosevelt Road in Little Rock that physicians there sent him to the hospital in Fayetteville. A bearded pathologist there, quick to recognize the talents of a genuine goldbrick, recommended Henry for a pension of something like fifty dollars a month. Henry hasn't seen the inside of a hospital since then.

Civility, her eyes still so hopelessly crossed that moderns are beginning to wonder how she sees anything at all, takes in washing and ironing. People like me — and there are some several dozen of us — remember that she nursed our parents when we were away, and because some of us have prospered, so has Civility's washing and ironing business. Indeed, it is really a laundry now.

According to Windy, Civility made the gown in which Momma was buried. She also nursed Momma through that last wild bout of insanity. When she is questioned about it, she is faintly amused. "That momma of yours jist couldn't git it in her head that you were really fighting a war."

Perhaps Charleston's real

understanding of Civility came in 1956. The country had begun to wonder about the Legion because there were Legionaires who burned books, not because they had read them but because they had looked at the titles, which they called "The Captions." Not the Post at Charleston. During that year Windy, an old man now and really not long for this world, saw to it that Civility was elected head of the Ladies Auxiliary.

Nobody ever found anything to honor Henry. He wasn't much, anyhow.

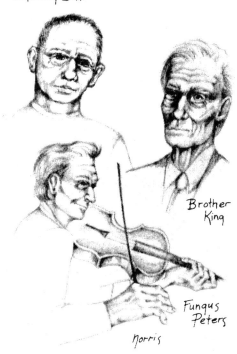

Charley Boxx

Brother King

Fungus Peters

Norris

XV

Fungus Peters, Charley Boxx, and Brother King were three of those minor characters who appeared during the lonely days of the Depression and in one way or another helped us get shed of some of the loneliness by which our lives abided.

Fungus Peters appeared in Charleston at the bottom of the Depression. He carried a toolbox and nothing else. The clothes he wore were clean, but there were grease stains that could never be removed from them. His hands, huge and callused, had been victims of his trade so long that they would never be clean again. He was an automobile mechanic. We paid no particular attention to his name; during the Depression, we didn't know what a fungus was, but we did know what peters were.

Fungus was walking when he came to Charleston. It was a hot day, and any kind of motion at all was an exercise in terror. Not to Fungus. He moved briskly and he didn't sweat.

We didn't ask questions of such men as Fungus. He was carrying a toolbox; thus he was a working man, likely to be honest. A loafer might make it a week in Charleston, but nobody would speak to him; he wouldn't stay long. A man looking for work might even have a past, but we didn't concern ourselves too much with what had happened somewhere else.

Fungus asked directions and Windy Spears sent him to Wilhite's Garage. Grover Wilhite was one of those bumbling silences who make fumbling plans for the future long after the future is already here and the past is an accident best forgotten. He was a blacksmith and he was preparing for the obvious, because there were a lot of Model A's and Model T's in Charleston by this time. Three farmers in Franklin County, south of the river, had already abanoned mules in favor of Farmall tractors.

But Grover Wilhite was no mechanic. When a car was brought in for repair he dismantled it, and when he found a part that fell in two in his hands, he welded it back together. He was never really able to understand why he couldn't make a car run again, so when Fungus appeared at his shop Grover made a firm effort to scramble out of his bumbling silence. "I cain't commence hollering about money till I find out what kind of cash your work puts in the box."

"I'm the best mechanic *this* state ever had." Fungus had kind of a different accent, as if perhaps he might have spent a couple of weeks in, say, California.

"That so?"

Fungus pointed to a couple of Model A's

sitting behind the shop. The white one belonged to Brother King, the Methodist preacher, and the other one belonged to Charley Boxx, who had just married Old Cat Murphy.

"How they act?"

Grover put his hand on Brother King's car. "Starts right up, cackles like a little red hen, then in about twenty minutes it slows down and finally stops."

Fungus peered first at the gas cap, then at the radiator cap. He switched them. "Crank 'er up. She'll run till she's out of gas."

Charley Boxx's Model A was something else. It took ten minutes to solve that problem. Somebody had pissed in the gas tank. "Drain it all out and clean the carburetor; it'll run."

Fungus was hired. He slept in the shop. There was a half-loft and the forge had left a lot of soot there, but Fungus didn't mind. He was one of those men who was somehow clean even if most of his hours were black with grease and grime. Grover didn't mind either; now he had both a mechanic and a night watchman.

And business picked up. There seemed to be no question Fungus couldn't answer about cars. A woman driving a Cord with Illinois license plates stalled on the Street one day. She looked at Charleston, murmured "My God," and then began looking for a mechanic to work on the most exotic of all American cars. Fungus somehow knew about some eccentricity in the Cord's ignition system and the car was running again within minutes. Will Bumpers owned a 1929 Dodge, dark brown with huge showcase windows and wailing brakes, never a really good car, but with a tinkering here and an adjustment somewhere else Fungus kept that old car running until Mr. Bumpers bought, used, a 1933 Chevrolet. Pendergrass & Flanagan, the Ford dealers, tried to hire Fungus away, but he wasn't interested.

There wasn't really a lot of work to do. Sometimes he was unemployed for as long as three days at a stretch, but that wasn't too often, because his work was good and his price was right. Both were guaranteed. There were people in town who wouldn't allow anybody else to open the hoods on their cars. There were even people in Fort Smith, our mecca, twenty-three miles away, who brought their Pierce-Arrows and Hudsons to Fungus, usually on a Saturday morning, because even if the cars were running like Singer sewing machines, Fungus gave them his serious attention.

When Fungus had nothing else to do he made fiddles. That's what he called them. He used several blocks of walnut, and with a kind of energetic patience he went to work. He roughed them out with a saw, the ordinary carpenter's tool, and then he whittled them down with a pocketknife. The final touches were done with the edge of a piece of glass; Fungus didn't like the sound of sandpaper. He sold the finished product for ten dollars.

It seemed that the fiddle buyers were all of a kind. They were men who wore big hats, chewed tobacco, talked loud, cussed a lot, and played for any one or more of the dozens of hillbilly bands that abounded on radio during the Depression. They showed up, sawed a few hoedowns on first one fiddle and then another, and after paying up, they left. None of us ever heard one of them say anything kind or generous about Fungus's fiddles, but they all sent their friends back to Fungus. Because some of them played for some pretty rough country dancings, they bought more fiddles than might be imagined.

Nobody knew where the peculiar stranger came from. Charley Boxx brought him in, said he'd spent the night at the hotel. Nobody had ever seen anything like that stranger before. His clothes, for one thing. We had seen them in the movies at the Gem Theater, but none of us actually believed that men really wore clothes like those in front of other people. He was a sissy, for another thing. When he brushed past me, I got a good sniff of a perfume I later learned to identify as Chanel No. 5. Charleston had only one sissy, an elephant of a boy so fat he would have to be a sissy because he would never be able to outrun a girl, so we didn't know a whole lot about the technique used in handling one in a conversation.

His accent wasn't right, either. Indeed,

as we listened to him talk, it began to occur first to Top, then to me, that this man wasn't an American. Windy became nervous, perhaps because he thought we would expect him to recognize anything that wasn't native to our shores, so to make sure, Windy headed home for his noon eats.

"Are you the gentleman who manufactures violins?" No voice had ever sounded so wrong in a blacksmith shop before.

There was an awful silence. It was a Saturday morning and a lot of us liked to loaf here because that gave us a chance to look under the hood of a Pierce-Arrow. I glanced at Top, and we sort of nodded to show each other that we could wait this one out; nobody would trouble us for this.

But Fungus was busy; he had no time for nuances. " 'Spect so."

"May I examine them?"

"Help yourself, boy." Fungus nodded to Grover, "Hand me that seven-sixteenths you got in your hand."

The stranger looked around. The shop was an entirely nonreflecting black because it had been a blacksmith shop so long before it had become a garage. Wearing those clothes, that stranger probably thought that over. Or perhaps it was us; among us were a half-dozen tobacco-chewers and almost as many snuff-dippers.

"Where *are* the violins?"

Fungus was instinctively a polite man, but he was a busy one too, and his auto work came first. "Just crawl up them steps there. The platform next to the skylight? All right, the fiddles're hanging on the walls up there."

Watching his hands on the rungs of the ladder, the stranger ascended into what must have been a sooty nightmare to him. Neither Fungus nor Grover paused, but the rest of us lost interest in the Pierce-Arrow. Almost five minutes passed, then we heard music we had never heard before. Oh, of course Ray Cravens, when he came to CHS and began teaching real music, played records for us, but nobody had ever heard anything like this before except when it was recorded.

Even Fungus stopped working a few

minutes to listen. Sitting there on the carbon dust of the shop's floor, Fungus had the look of a man who has suddenly heard the sound of a perfect engine. He nodded, replete with satisfaction, and then he nodded again, but there was work to be done on the Pierce-Arrow and he wasn't the sort who loafed.

When the stranger climbed back down the steps from the loft, he was carrying with him every fiddle Fungus had in stock. Top and I sprang forward and politely helped him to the ground. He looked at us as if perhaps he were wondering whether we were going to attack him, or maybe he even wondered what we would be doing in a dirty little old town like this, and then he nodded his thanks. He didn't look quite so sissy now.

"There are seven violins here," the stranger said.

Bewildered, Fungus put his tools away. "Aw hell, man, this's a Saturday morning. You orta've picked the fiddle you want and left the others up there. I ain't got time to wag 'em up myself."

For a moment the stranger was

confused. "Oh no, I will buy all of them from you."

Fungus finally understood. "Oh." Or he thought he understood. "You a bandleader, ain't you?"

The stranger didn't understand at all, but he was willing to try. "Perhaps you would call me a bandleader, yes. May I offer you a price for the instruments?"

"You a bandleader, all right; that's the only way to explain them clothes you wearing." Fungus sniffed. "And that shaving lotion you use."

"May I offer you a price?"

Fungus was pleased, but he shook his head. "I don't bargain on my fiddles. I get a straight ten dollars a fiddle. If that don't suit you, haul 'em right back up them steps."

"Oh no!" The stranger was quick to say that. "That — that suits me." And the stranger produced the cash. He didn't carry a bullcod; it was a billfold of a design we had never seen before. And in it was the damnedest wad anybody in Charleston, Arkansas, had ever seen. He shucked out seventy dollars and left, crawling into a foreign car of some kind driven by a black man; he was gone.

We talked about that for the remainder of the afternoon. Charley Boxx, not busy at the hotel until the serving of supper approached, came down to the shop and talked about his reaction when the stranger appeared at the hotel. We listened until Charley had to leave.

Top and I walked back up the Street with Charley. We liked him. Almost everybody in Charleston liked Charley. He was a compact man, full at the chest and broad at the shoulder, but as Windy said, Charley was built a little close to the ground. Once he had been our boozer, our bounder; it was said a few years ago that a girl who dated Charley Boxx had better settle on a man not up to the standards set by the girl's mother, because her reputation was ruined.

Charley owned a Model A, which he had once painted purple, and until he married Old Cat that car careened around all over town on a Saturday night, Charley at the wheel, drunker than a hoot owl, singing at the top of his lungs. Because he sometimes stopped in at Spread Benefield's cobbler shop during the noon hour, he liked the gospel, so when he was drunk, Charley sang shaped notes, "Bringing in the Sheaves."

Charley was a painter by trade. Houses, signs, barns, privies; during the Depression not many people used paint, and Charley would paint anything it would stick to. His pay was good, three dollars a day and the cost of the paint, and Windy mused that Charley might have a little green stashed back. But if he did, it wasn't in the bank. Since Burl McIntosh had left town, Charley didn't really trust banks.

He was polite to everybody, even Clyde Hiatt, president of the bank, but there were things and people and attitudes Charley Boxx didn't trust. He liked Scrooge Wilkins because they both enjoyed vegetables. He got along with Windy and Spread, and of course with Top and with me. But the only persons he trusted were Will Bumpers and Brother King, both for the same reason.

Charley Boxx was a drinking man. Not

a drunk. He got drunk only on a Saturday night, and even then there was nothing sullen or bitter or mean with him; he drove about town, sometimes with the daughter of an Onion Creek rowdy, and he was always singing and he always sang the gospel. When he finally had all he wanted to drink, he drove home and put himself to bed. He owned a little two-roomer just east of Jenkins Woods. On a Saturday night he left his Coleman lamp burning until he awakened the next day.

He never asked anybody to join him in his drinking. The girls who dared go out with him were carefully chosen; he wanted nothing to do with a drinking woman. Indeed, there were people who had never seen him drink at all, not even beer; he wasn't a public man. People liked him; children, dogs, and young people. He sometimes dated Toy, the waitress at the Tourist Cafe, but she took up with Melmer Dunmore, and nobody wanted anything to do with a woman who was willing to be seen publicly with Melmer. Daughters and sisters of Onion Creek rowdies, anxious to move up to the society of Charleston, were the only ones regularly seen with Charley Boxx.

Thus until he became acquainted with Old Cat, his life didn't vary much. He knew her, of course; everybody knew Old Cat. But he had never spoken a word to her until one frigid night when it seemed that the drive to his two-roomer was more than he wanted to try. Ice lay over the town like a shroud. Charley decided to spend the night at the hotel.

He sobered up in the lobby. For almost an hour he could hardly more than blubber, but he wouldn't drink either. Along past midnight, he was sober enough that he could talk. Old Cat plied him with coffee, and soon enough he could speak as many as eight words at a time. By two o'clock Old Cat was teaching him to dance. Perhaps she liked the chore because her breasts, great but not monumental, struck him directly in the face. Except to pack his things, Charley never returned to his two-roomer.

They were married one dewy night that spring. "I ain't much, Cat, but if you marry me, I'll never lay lip on a bottle of booze long's I live."

The county clerk, a hot-tempered old woman with a red mole on her chin and a long white hair sprouting from that mole, was rustled out of bed, and because there was no cooling-off period in Arkansas in 1938, the wedding license was issued. The justice of the peace, J. P. Jones, wouldn't get out of bed after midnight, so the lovers went to Brother King.

Brother King gave Charley a lecture concerning bottled spirits and Charley promised total abstinence. They were married.

The next we saw of them, they were seated in rockers on the front porch of the hotel. They were holding bottles of Dr. Pepper. Somehow or other, they looked younger. Charley closed his two-roomer and moved into the hotel. There was a three-room suite on the second floor. We settled down to await developments.

We were disappointed. There were no more Saturday night singings or careenings. Charley and Cat drank Dr. Pepper, sometimes Coke. There was a kind of splendid serenity in their lives;

they spent a lot of time on the hotel's porch, holding hands and rocking, and they seemed to enjoy watching the placid passage of the history of Charleston during the Depression.

There must have been a thousand bums pass through Charleston that spring. They invariably tracked to the hotel, something they had never done before, and sure enough, Old Cat and Charley fed them at the back door, where a couple of picnic tables were set up on that patch of bermuda just behind the hotel. Old Cat wouldn't allow the bums inside because she didn't want her paying guests to know she was giving as much quantity and as much quality to the people who had no money at all.

Sometimes, when he wasn't busy in the hotel, Charley sat at the picnic tables and talked to the bums. None of us ever knew what he talked to them about. Somehow or other, we never figured it was any of our business. Except for Brother King, who called regularly, none of us knew anything at all about that life that passed at the hotel.

One day Old Cat died. She went to the bank to deposit the week's receipts because Charley wouldn't agree to do business there. Then she went to the Creasant Drug Store to take care of a little charge account she kept there. Nadine Potts, sixty-seven and in charge of the fountain since she was sixteen, the day the fountain was installed, noticed that Old Cat wasn't looking well. Old Cat made it across the Street and into the Hardware, where she paid Will Bumpers the two-dollars-odd she'd owed him since the previous Saturday. She looked up at Mr. Bumpers, trusting him for the same reason that she trusted Brother King, and then she said something like, "Mr. Bumpers, I'm fixing to die. You be sure people're nice to old Charley." And then, as easily as that, Old Cat did die.

It took us almost two hours to decide who would tell Charley. Finally, we chose the obvious; he had married them and there would be nobody else but Brother King. Top and I were sent to the Methodist parsonage. Brother King was there, grumbling about something he was reading in *The Upper Room*. He removed his dentures from his pocket and put them where they belonged. "Dead, you say?"

"Yes sir."

Brother King nodded a couple of times. "All right. Top, you go on back to the funeral home and tell 'em I've gone to the hotel." He took my arm. "You come on and go with me; I might need the help of somebody young."

"Yes sir."

Brother King was a massive man and his hand on my shoulder was heavy, but it seemed to belong there. He kept it there until he briskly crossed the lobby. He was old, almost ninety, but he was moving rapidly. Just as he reached the door to the kitchen he paused, and moments were required for me to understand that he was praying. Brother King nodded to me; he was ready.

Charley's face didn't change much, but any change at all on a Charleston face was noticeable. "Cat's late and you'd not be here if everything was all right."

Brother King placed a massive arm

about Charley's shoulders. "It's the worst, Charley."

Charley placed his face against Brother King's chest, much the way children do, and almost a minute passed before he stood away. "I've been telling 'er she wasn't feeling right."

"I'll turn my back, Charley," Brother King said, "and you take you a drink."

"No sir, I quit drinking the night you married us." Charley removed his apron. "Where's she at, Brother King?"

"Funeral home." Brother King picked up the apron. "You go on. The boy and I'll finish peeling these potatoes."

It was Windy Spears who was waiting on the porch of the hotel, and together, both deep in grief, they walked to the funeral home. There were several people standing about, although on another day they would have all been at home, sitting down for supper. They all spoke to Charley and Windy, aware that the two men were equally grieved. At the funeral home they hesitated. Charley paced a few times and Windy sat on the curb.

Finally it was Will Bumpers who made

it bearable. The funeral home was an adjunct of the Hardware, and thus Mr. Bumpers, even if he did grieve at the death of those people he had known all his life, knew how to keep himself in hand. He brought out three rockers and installed them on the porch of the funeral home. He sat with charley and Windy and they rocked placidly throughout the night. Perhaps as many as three hundred people came by that night, murmured things they hoped were comforting, then went on home. When the body was transferred to the church the next day, the rocking chairs went along too.

Brother King, when he preached the funeral, didn't quite know what to say. Old Cat was a wildcat, wife of a boozer, but she had died in grace and Brother King reckoned that was enough, and that was the kind of sermon it was. It would have been easier if he had been a young man in Charleston, but he was past retirement age before he had even laid eyes on the town. He had come here because the Methodists splintered.

Methodists don't splinter, the legend

says. It's the Baptists. But in 1931 the Methodists in Charleston did act as if they were going to splinter. They disagreed on politics, and because that was a good year for politicians, they had a lot to argue about. There was talk about founding a new church, to be called Wesley Memorial, of course, and that would surely have happened if the Bishop hadn't put a stop to it. He sent Henry King to Charleston.

Brother King wasn't one of those sweet reasonable preachers who seem as close to selling a new car as they do a way to Heaven. He was a roaring hell-raiser. When he preached his first sermon from our pulpit he stood there, his voice roaring, and gave us hell for a solid hour. "And just to make it hurt a little more, let's take up another collection."

He couldn't have brought if off if he hadn't been so old. In 1931 he was eighty-five, twenty years past the retirement age of Methodist preachers. But he was the best man in the sanctuary, and every once in a while he said so: "If you don't like what you hear from this pulpit, step right up after church and we'll settle our differences under the bell tower." That invariably prompted his wife, a waif of a woman with a child's voice that somehow carried well, to say, "Now Henry . . ." And Brother King was quick to apologize — to her. "Oh, sorry, honey, I forgot."

He had been a circuit rider all his life, and that was a breed of men whose subtleties had been ground away by congregations much rougher than even, say, could have been found in the Onion Creek Township.

The first couple of months of his tenure were ragged. He preached a sermon allowing that there were people who were going to drink and not much could be done toward stopping them; therefore, beer should be legal because it wasn't likely to do so much damage. "I've drunk the fool stuff and I'd rather feed it to the pigs, but it's not strong enough to kill you. They say it's hard to get drunk on the stuff because you get so much exercise going back and forth to the privy." The Methodist board, gray-headed to a man with the exception of Will Bumpers, grumbled and finally agreed, unanimously, that he shouldn't have said that. Brother King came right back: "To use a perfectly good theological term, go to hell."

They didn't go. They didn't need to; there was plenty of hell in his sermons.

Brother King even went to the movies. Charleston Methodists went to the movies, with exceptions not worthy of mention, but they didn't think their preacher should. Jim Tom Abernathy even arose during Announcements and asked if the preacher really intended to go see another talkie. "When Will Rogers makes a talkie, I go see it. Now you people get something straight: I'm a human being. I have a serious fault: I like to have fun."

"Now Henry . . ."

"Honey, you hush and let me finish."

"All right, Henry."

"I've lived so long and I've been in such close proximity to Methodists and their sins that I'm bound to have enough faults to be a Baptist, so leave me alone, and if my sins send me to hell, wait around and we'll talk old times."

Jim Tom Abernathy was one of those men occasionally found near so many hundreds of tiny Arkansas towns during the Depression, grim, silent by instinct, puzzled by the present, relieved to be shed of the past, suspicious of the future. He was tall, even taller than Brother King, and there was a certain shamble to his walk that made people say he looked like a young actor, Henry Fonda, who was becoming popular. Jim Tom was a farmer, a good one too, and his skin was burned almost black by that sizzling sun that somehow makes vegetables and flowers grow. His wife was a big woman, quiet to the point of silence, but there was a quality that caused men to stare at her. She let Jim Tom do the talking; thus the Abernathy house was almost silent. The half-dozen sons, Matthew, Mark, Luke, John, Job, and Peter, were varying copies of their father. The solitary daughter, Naomi Ruth, looked as if she might be her mother's younger sister.

"Don't you ever go to the movies, Mr. Abernathy?"

"No sir, Preacher, I don't."

"Why not? They're not *all* sinful."

Another man might have rigged a lie and dumped it out, and there was certainly a tradition of lying in Charleston, but Jim Tom had never learned. "I go to bed at dark and get up at daylight."

For a moment Brother King's wrathful old face relaxed and the congregation caught a glimpse of a man who had an enormous capacity for tenderness; then the hellfire returned, and for the time being, at least, he was through talking about the movies.

Somehow the two men became friends. Jim Tom was a loner, both by instinct and by preference; he liked the company of his silent sons, that daughter, and that wife; others made him nervous. So it was kind of a jolt to all of us when Brother King, his wife, and the entire Abernathy family met at the Creasant Drug Store for ice cream one Saturday afternoon. The two men and the six boys sat around one table, a rounded slab of polished marble supported by fancifully twisted bars of steel, and the two wives and the daughter sat at another table. Jim Tom and the boys simply grinned, those somehow delightful grins of men who are habitually expressionless, and Brother King talked. He said nothing funny, but, prompted by their father, the boys occasionally laughed. The laughter always ended abruptly. The women giggled twice. I am unable to record what Brother King said because it wasn't important enough to overwhelm the thing we call time, but I do remember that Methodism wasn't mentioned at all.

When they rose to leave, Jim Tom paused to study the refrigerator in which Hooty Sturdy stored the ice cream. Outside, they stood in the hot sun to say their goodbyes. The Abernathy family climbed silently into that wagon that had been rigged as a surrey, but Jim Tom waited on the ground, his head down in that gesture some men can use to get attention.

"First time we ever had any store-bought ice cream." Jim Tom wasn't confessing. He was merely passing on information he thought of interest.

"I was in my seventies before I had my first taste of it." Brother King nodded vigorously. "I like it, but there's nothing quite so good as a freezer full of good home-made stuff."

"Mmm." That meant Jim Tom wasn't through. "That freezer in there . . ."

"Keeps it from melting." Brother King was a patient man and he was in no hurry.

"If it'll keep cream that long, looks like a man could put up a lot of eats without having to go through all that canning." Jim Tom nodded slowly. "A kitchen gets awful hot of a summer."

"Hot as hell," Brother King said loudly.

And the two men stood there in that terrible sun and grinned at each other. It occurred to me, twenty years later, that these men were playing the zenith of the roles in life their temperaments had devised for them.

The next day, Jim Tom and Brother King appeared at the drugstore without their families, but they didn't order ice cream. They spoke to Hotty Sturdy, who furnished them the name of the freezer's maker. Jim Tom wrote a letter, found a price, and ordered two of the machines, one for his house and one for the parsonage. Mr. Slim, a Baptist, filled it with blanched vegetables. That fall, when pork and beef were butchered by Jim Tom, it was refilled with meat.

Brother King remained. By 1939, when we were beginning to hope that the Depression was going to be over, we had begun to accept him not as a friend but as an essential discomfort. Towns of 853 people need that. He nagged us, fumed, roared, threatened, visited our sick, performed our marriages, and preached our funerals.

He was eighty-nine when his wife died. He buried her himself, and as he stood there in the pulpit, wild and craggy and crushed too, and recited the facts of her life in a wan little voice that moved us beyond tears, for the first time some of us understood that death is a tragedy only to the living.

''She never bore me a baby; God didn't intend her to. She knew I never loved another woman; God fixed it that way. She was seventy years old before she even rode on a train, so she didn't do much except make the kind of wife a preacher can't —" He stopped. He tried several times to go on, but the throat was too old.

Jim Tom, moving with that somehow reassuring shamble of his, clad in the same black suit he had worn to church since his father had given it to him on his twentieth birthday thirty years ago, his sun-blackened skin somehow native to this sanctuary — Jim Tom shambled down the aisle and placed himself at Brother King's elbow. Brother King nodded, rather convulsively, and Jim Tom touched his shoulder, and Brother King finished the sentence: "— the wife a preacher can't always have but always hopes for."

His preaching softened after that because there was no waif in the congregation to call him down when he stepped out too far ahead of us. The Bishop came to hear him preach once and then ordered him retired, but a deputation, headed by Will Bumpers, waited upon the Bishop, and after a long hour's pleading, Brother King was reassigned to Charleston.

I spoke to Brother King the night before I left for my military duty. He explained to me, in terms perhaps having nothing at all to do with the Trinity, why my mother's insanity had been something I tried to ignore.

"I'm told she was a handsome woman, intelligent. She's still the only woman in Charleston with a college education. Do you remember your father?"

"No sir."

"He was a physician, wasn't he?"

"Yes sir."

"He died when you were two?"

"Yes sir."

"You've never heard a bad thing about him, have you?"

"No sir."

"But you've heard your mother talking crazy hate all your life."

"Yes sir."

"Human nature," Brother King said. "It's that simple. You've been unhappy all your life, so you wish it had been your mother to die and your father to live."

Brother King may have been right; I don't know. He buried my mother. Miss

Doll and Miss Hettie somehow learned that he had written down every word he planned to say at the funeral. They tried to make him believe that they should keep the sermon for me, but Brother King would have none of that. "It might give him a little pleasant pain now, but twenty years from now, when he's old enough to understand how lucky he was to have lived in Charleston, my sermon's gonna sound kind of empty." He burned that sermon in Doc Bollinger's fireplace.

Brother King lived until the war was over. The day he died was a stifling one; a thunderstorm was growling in the southwest. I was in Fayetteville. They told me he was seated in his rocker, which had been installed on the front porch of the parsonage in May and wouldn't be taken inside until October. He was working on his sermon. People had worried about him because he had recently preached the funeral sermon of Will Bumpers and he had not really recovered from the ordeal. One of his neighbors heard him grumble, but that didn't attract much attention; he did that when he was working on a hot sermon, and this was the kind of a day he would have written a hot one.

Then he put his head back, and after a few moments his rocker was still. He didn't drop his pencil, nor did his hand let the sermon go. The Bishop, a younger man who had been a chaplain during the war and was likely to be more than merely sentimental about these old circuit riders, preached the funeral; he simply read the sermon Brother King had been working on. It was about like the others he had preached since 1931.

Those are the essentials of his life in Charleston. It only remains to note that he left a will. Jim Tom Abernathy was the executor. When the will was probated, it was valued at a dollar and twenty-seven cents. Brother King left it all to the Hymnal Fund.

XVI

By Christmas 1939 the war in Europe was almost four months old, and even if we hated to think it was the cure for the Depression, we knew it was true. We didn't say it, not even in those privacies in which simple truths can be uttered. It simply seemed reasonable that the Depression should end soon. The Dust Bowl was gone too; no longer was our tall blue sky turned yellow by somebody else's dirt. Eight years had been a long time.

But the Depression had remained. Indeed, perhaps because it had taken so long to reach Arkansas from that mystery called the East, it might last a little longer here. There were still hungry people in Charleston during the winter of 1939. Some of them hadn't been able to afford the fruit jars to can vegetables in. Others were too proud for Relief. Some had been found ineligible for WPA because a senseless bureaucrat didn't like the looks of their application papers.

We buried the last of the Pickering old maids that November. Doc Bollinger took them food and so did Will Bumpers, but those two women were the daughters of Captain Pickering and they had their pride. Nobody around here reminded them anymore that Captain Pickering had been a carpetbagger, not a Confederate. When Doc Bollinger filled out the death certificate, he noted that they had died of pneumonia. Doc was that kind of man; he enjoyed being that kind of man.

Unproductive milch cows and overage boars were still being butchered for meat after the first frost of that year. The meat was canned because it would have been tough to the degree of being unchewable if it hadn't been subjected to the tenderizing of great heat and vacuum in those Mason jars.

We were still afraid to define the future, because we didn't want to uncover a truth we didn't like. We all knew, for instance, that the schools weren't going to stay open the full nine months. We hoped for seven months. Our teachers were paid forty dollars a month, but they were paid by warrant, which meant that they actually received less than thirty dollars. The bank examiners, when they called, said as little as possible about those loans due for call. The bank would extend the loans, because that was just about all it could do; the bank wasn't in the real estate business.

We didn't even hope for a Christmas parade. This year, it just couldn't happen. Even during the year the Bank of South Franklin closed, there had been a Christmas parade. We had always had it, but not this year. The city council met in the store rooms of the Star Barber Shop and a lot of things were discussed. Aimlessly. Nobody mentioned a Christmas parade.

Parents took the same approach. Children dreamed their private dreams. None of us seriously hoped. Topwater hitchhiked to Fort Smith and managed to steal a silver spoon from a jewelry store. He gave it to me so I could give it to Momma. I knew that I would awaken on Christmas morning just as I had always awakened — my Christmas was what I made it — but there were children who still clung to hope. Most of them would find their stockings filled with perhaps a couple of baked sweet potatoes. Some might even find an orange.

That was the way it stood on December the fifteenth. It turned cold that night, but there was a quality in the weather that didn't thrill or prompt us toward a hope for a white Christmas. It was a dry cold, windy, even dusty.

Nobody ever found who organized the miracle of Christmas 1939. Somehow, tons of fried chicken appeared, so Miss Hettie had something to do with it. Those thousands of oranges must have come from J. O. Cone and Claude Jones, our grocers. There was a general nothing store in town. It was owned by a Pole, but because he was a Catholic, he was called Fritz Schumke; he put a little toy in the mesh bags with the fried chicken and the orange. Doc Bollinger probably financed the buying of the crooked candy. There's no telling.

The parade itself simply happened. Windy thought it might look good if some of the boys from the Legion Post stood around in uniform on our three street corners. There was nothing for them to do, except perhaps stand at attention for anybody who might ask them to do so. The Charleston Tigers Band had new uniforms, made by three pairs of hands at the sewing machines, and those uniforms needed to be seen. Dock Frye had recently secured the draft concession for Falstaff in Charleston, and he wanted to build a float advertising as much. Scrooge Wilkins spent several days making a papier-mâché hotdog, which he mounted on a Model T he had found somewhere.

There were hundreds of people who wanted to see a parade. Most of them also wanted to participate in one. There is no telling how the rumor began: the parade was going to take place, after all; it would probably happen on the afternoon of the twenty-second. Nobody confessed to the selection of the date. Nobody even said the parade was going to happen at all.

But it did.

The band was the development of Barney Stittchen, telegrapher at the depot. He was not a bandsman; he was shaped notes. But he organized the band, and for several years the Legion paid the bills. When Mr. Pennypacker left and the new superintendent could see a band in the future of the public schools, it was taken over by a man named Ray Cravens, imported for the job, and it became the Charleston Tigers Band. When Cravens got through with it, the band not only could march, it could play too.

The band led the parade that year. All the traditional Christmas hymns were played, but they were played as marches.

Because there was nothing else to do, the bank marched and countermarched and did the few stunts Cravens had taught it. There were twenty-eight of us in that band, and there was no doubt that it was the grandest thing *this* town had ever seen.

Immediately behind the band was Santa Claus. It was Spread, of course. It had always been Spread. Seated around him were the four children he had adopted from the last orphans bus, and they were singing "Shout the Glad Tidings." That Santa looked like a Santa. The four children were dressed as little Santas.

Then Scrooge Wilkins. That hotdog was beautiful. It was the wrong color, a little brown, but it was beautiful. His face gentle, his smile soft, he was tossing candy into the audience.

Dock Frye's Falstaff float, an ordinary farm wagon drawn by a span of mules driven by John Frank Spiller, was just that and that's all. Dock himself sat on the bench in front of his cafe. He was munching Limburger and sipping Falstaff. Nobody wondered then and perhaps nobody wonders now, but Dock drank a lot of Falstaff and ate a lot of Limburger without ever becoming fatter than a fishing pole.

Miss Hettie had bought a new Ford touring car, and because we all wanted to see her, she let the top down and drove it in the parade. She looked beautiful. Miss Hettie was the only pretty woman Charleston ever had.

There were others. Indeed, before the afternoon was over, the parade moved up and down the Street some six times, which gave some of us a chance to drop out while others took their turn at marching.

Windy didn't drop out. He had always been the parade marshal. It was a chilly day and Windy's nose was running, but he didn't use his bandana. He sniffed. He paced along, his ancient Army shoes brisk on WPA pavement, and somehow or other Windy was almost the entire parade. That campaign hat, later to become famous as the headgear of Smokey the Bear; that high-collared tunic; those olive-drab wrappings about his calves: it was the full

263

uniform of the soldier of World War I, the World's War. And the rifle. Good God, yes, the rifle. It was the 1903 Springfield. It seemed that every veteran had somehow managed to steal one of them when he got out of the Army in 1918. It was a political institution, that rifle.

But so was Windy. If Mark Twain had lived long enough, he would have recognized Windy as a natural brother. Indeed, our twentieth-century Mark Twain, Will Rogers, should have attended that parade.

Even after the parade was over, Windy wasn't allowed to go on about his business. He was hurrahed on to the courthouse, and on the steps there he stood, sniffing, his bladder killing him, but he went through the manual of arms with a kind of hope that was the final, really truthful end to the parade. He was the other idol.

EPILOGUE

The trees have come back to Nixon Cemetery. That hodgepodge of monuments and stones lay in a long green shade when I was a boy, and even during that drought of the early thirties when dust was blown out of Oklahoma and Texas and onto us, those trees lived. They weren't killed until the drought of 1954.

That was a peculiar tragedy to me. All of those remarkable people lying in that cool green shade were, in the passage of months, exposed to a sun so brilliant that natives of other states are unable to believe our summers are what they are. Topwater's tomb, polished white marble, always looked right and good in the shadow of the huge black oak over it, but when that tree died and was removed before it fell, the tombstone was so bright that it was painful to the eyes.

It took a long time for me to get over it when, in the name of wartime patriotism, the Confederate cannons were given away as vital metals. After all, I had outgrown my vague romance with the Confederates. But when those trees died, I cried. It seemed to me that those names so important to my youth were exposed to a light from which they had been safely hidden. There were black oaks and white oaks and red oaks and willow oaks and Sherman oaks, redbuds, dogwoods, shads, hickories. Huge things, virgin growth, some so broadly buttressed that they were spilling over the oldest tombstones as if bark and wood had inexplicably melted and hardened again.

That was how dry the earth became, baked a hundred feet beneath the surface so dry that the roots of even those timeless monuments couldn't find water.

As frequently as I could, when the rains came back to Arkansas, I returned to plant trees. My children, learning to walk and easily amused, played on the tombstones as if they had suddenly found an amusement park untouched by noise and littering. As much as possible, I planted the same kinds of trees I remembered, but nurseries don't stock all of the oaks that had once grown there.

When I went back the next spring, my gardening equipment again in hand, I noticed that I wasn't the only one desperate about the trees. Spread Benefield's twin daughters, one of whom was pregnant and worried about it because she thought she was too old to bear children, had been to that stand of hardwoods near Tater Hill Run and had found black oak seedlings. One of Will Bumpers's sons had found some Sherman oak acorns and planted them in pots, and now there were trees big enough to plant.

For years, that ridge remained barren when it was seen from Highway 22, but it has recently begun to change. A hundred years will pass before it again begins to resemble the cemetery we remembered. But Decoration Day is no longer so dismal.

We meet there on the first Sunday afternoon in May. The crowd is a rather large one, and, interestingly enough, there are quite a few young people. They've heard of the Depression, and they're getting sick of hearing that a dollar a day was the best price a man could get for his day's work, but they pause when a parent will suddenly straighten from a rosebush or a seedling and gaze unbelievingly at those jumbles of stones and murmur, "We stuck together. Nothing, nobody came between us."

The bodies of most of our war dead have been brought home. Some couldn't be found. They're buried beneath those things middle-aged veterans took to calling "G.I. tombstones." There are special monuments to Topwater Mulligan and Thumb Holyfield because they both won the Medal of Honor, but we have been satisfied with that flat stone with name, rank, and organization embossed into its surface. There is a sameness about them, and we ordinarily wouldn't like that, but they're simple and honest and we think they're things of unusual beauty.

After four hours of hard work, the cemetery looks good enough that we're satisfied for another year. The hymnals are brought out and we sing. Almost all of us middle-aged ones sing shaped notes rather than lines-and-spaces, but we haven't passed our gift onto our children. The hymns are the old ones, the same ones heard in country churches for better than a hundred years, and some of them have words likely to curdle the imagination if spoken or put on paper. Young people, almost amused but touched too, smile because we are so old-fashioned, and there is a touch of pride in those faces too: we passed a test because we stuck together. Sometimes we imagine that our young ones even understand our materialism.

The Legion is still there but it isn't the same now. Its innocent pretense is gone, and not a man has saved his uniform so he can bring it out to show as Windy did. A few half-hearted lies are produced, but a lot of us are college-educated now, so we can read for entertainment. There is television too. Those sorts of things are hard on Legionaires and other liars.

At the end of the day, there is a picnic on the ground. And that is when I am convinced that Charleston, if it doesn't flourish, will certainly survive. Fried chicken, sliced ham, buttermilk, pork'n beans, and tons of tomatoes if spring comes early enough. Several of us, afraid the picnic committee will forget, bring a case of puppy-peckers.